THE LONG WAY HOME

ALSO BY ANDREW KLAVAN

The Last Thing I Remember

The Truth of the Matter

THE LONG WAY HOME

THE
HOMELANDERS

BOOK TWO

by
ANDREW KLAVAN

THOMAS NELSON
Since 1798

NASHVILLE   DALLAS   MEXICO CITY   RIO DE JANEIRO

Published in Nashville, Tennessee, by Thomas Nelson. Thomas Nelson is a registered trademark of Thomas Nelson, Inc.

Page design by Mandi Cofer.

Thomas Nelson, Inc., titles may be purchased in bulk for educational, business, fund-raising, or sales promotional use. For information, please e-mail SpecialMarkets@ThomasNelson.com.

Publisher's Note: This novel is a work of fiction. Names, characters, places, and incidents are either products of the author's imagination or used fictitiously. All characters are fictional, and any similarity to people living or dead is purely coincidental.

ISBN 978-1-59554-587-9 (trade paper)

Library of Congress Cataloging-in-Publication Data

Klavan, Andrew.
  The long way home / Andrew Klavan.
    p. cm. — (The Homelanders ; bk. 2)
  Summary: As eighteen-year-old Charlie West continues to elude the law and the group of terrorists looking for him, he tries to remember what happened a year ago and find out who has framed him so he can clear his name.
  ISBN 978-1-59554-713-2 (printed case hardcover)
  [1. Fugitives from justice—Fiction. 2. Amnesia—Fiction. 3. Terrorism—Fiction. 4. Adventure and adventurers—Fiction.] I. Title.
  PZ7.K67823Lo 2010
  [Fic]—dc22

                         2009034531

Printed in the United States of America
11 12 13 14 RRD 6 5 4 3 2 1

THIS BOOK IS FOR
TOM AND MARY BELLE SNOW.

PART ONE

CHAPTER ONE

The Killer in the Mirror

The man with the knife was a stranger. I never saw him before he tried to kill me.

I was in the Whitney Library when it happened, about seven miles from my hometown of Spring Hill. I'd been there for about forty-five minutes. I had come with a plan—a plan to clear my name, to get free, to get home to my family and out of danger. Now I had to leave. It wasn't safe for me to stay in any one place for very long.

I was in the main research room on the library's second floor. I went down the hall and pushed into the men's room. I took off my black fleece and hung it on the door of one of the stalls. Then, wearing just my jeans and black T-shirt, I stood at the sink and splashed cold water on my face.

I was tired—way tired. I had been on the road—on the run—I don't know—several weeks—a long time. I had to fight to stay alert. If I didn't stay alert, I wouldn't stay alive.

I dried myself off with a couple of paper towels. I looked at myself in the mirror. The guy looking back at me was six feet tall. Thin but with broad shoulders, good muscles, still in good shape. I had a lean, kind of solemn face with a mop of brown hair flopping over the forehead. Brown eyes—serious eyes—probably too serious for a guy who was only eighteen—but honest and straightforward. At least, I always thought they were . . .

I shook my head. *Snap out of it.* This was no time to doubt myself. I had to keep my spirits up, keep going. *Never give in.*

It was hard sometimes. I have to admit it. With the bad guys after me, and even the good guys—the police—after me too. It was hard not to get discouraged. Lonely. I missed my home. I missed my friends. I missed my mom and dad. I even missed my sister, who could be very annoying, believe me. Imagine sitting down to watch your absolutely favorite television show and just as it's about to begin, a nuclear explosion wipes out all of civilization as we know it—that's how annoying my sister could be. But I missed her anyway.

I missed just being a regular guy, just going to school and church and hanging out and doing regular things.

But it was no good thinking about that now. I had to keep going. I had to do what I'd come here to do. I'd promised myself I wouldn't stop trying. I'd promised God too. And I wouldn't stop. Not ever.

I turned away from the mirror. I took the fleece down from the stall door. I'd bought it at a thrift shop a few days ago. Something to keep me warm now that winter was coming. I tapped it to feel the papers folded up in the inside pocket. That's what I'd come to the library to find. I had what I wanted. It was time to go.

I slipped the fleece over my head, working my arms into the long sleeves.

It was just then—just as I got the fleece on—that the man came in.

He was a little older than I was—in his twenties maybe. A bit taller and a bit bigger around the waist and shoulders. He was wearing black jeans and a red windbreaker.

He had a round, clean, pleasant face. Blond hair, blue eyes. He looked like a nice guy. He gave me a quick nod as he entered and I nodded back. Then he moved past me, heading toward the urinals at the far end of the room.

I took a step away from him, toward the door, ready to leave. As I went, I glanced over at the mirror to check myself one last time. I lifted my fist to my reflection by way of encouragement. Never give in.

And, as I did that, I caught a glimpse of the man behind me. I saw his reflection, too, out of the corner of my eye. Strangely, he had stopped walking toward the urinals. He had pivoted around, back toward me.

Suddenly, without any warning at all, he had a knife in his hand. It was a killer's knife, a combat knife. A seven-inch blade of black steel.

At the very moment I spotted him in the mirror, he tried to plunge the blade into my spine.

A jolt of terror went through me, an electric panic that gave me almost supernatural speed. I leapt to my left, turning sideways. The blade lanced past my midsection, so close I felt its motion through the fleece. My years of karate training kicked in. I reacted without thinking, smacking his elbow with my left palm to push the knife hand away.

But I was moving so fast, in so much fear, I stumbled,

tripped over my own feet, and staggered back deeper into the bathroom.

That saved my life. Because the man with the knife was well-trained. He knew how to fight. He was already slashing backward at my face. If I hadn't stumbled away from him, he'd have cut my throat right there.

I let out a grunt, bending away from the blade. I still didn't have my feet under me, and the movement sent me even farther off balance. I fell, tumbling down to the floor.

It was the end of me. I was sure of it.

You have to understand: a trained man with a knife is as deadly as anything, even more dangerous in some ways than a man with a gun. You might grab a gun. You might wrestle it away. But you can't get hold of a knife without getting cut. And if the knife-man knows what he's doing, he can carve you up with a blade just as fast as a bullet.

And this guy knew what he was doing, all right. All the karate training in the world wasn't going to save me if I didn't act fast and act smart. If I fell and he came down on top of me, I'd be dead in seconds.

I knew it even as I was falling. The panic raced through my belly. The thoughts raced through my head: *I have to do something.*

I hit the tiled floor and kept rolling, fast, away from the oncoming killer. I rolled and leapt up, gaining my feet in the back of the bathroom, pressed up against the far wall, the urinals on either side of me.

Before I could even think, he was there, he was on me, driving the knife toward my gut, the black blade glinting in the light.

A cry escaped me in my desperation. I only just managed to leap out of the way, to grab his wrist with my two hands.

But I couldn't hold him. He yanked the knife back and if I hadn't let go, he would've slashed my fingers off. Immediately, he came at me again. His round, clean face was now a mask of fury. His blue eyes were full of death.

I was losing this fight. I knew it. It was only a matter of time before the knife slipped home. There was no way to overpower a trained assassin like this. No way to outfight him.

There was only one chance. I had to outthink him. Somehow, in my terror, in my panic, with murder hanging over me like a sword, I had to figure a way out.

The killer kept coming at me, the blade weaving before me like the head of a cobra. He kept the point in my eyes so I couldn't see it clearly, couldn't gauge the distance. He was forcing me toward the middle of the room, to where I'd be hemmed in between the stalls and the sinks with nowhere to move. I stepped backward quickly, waiting for the fatal strike.

Then, with snakelike swiftness, the strike came—and at the same time, there came a desperate thought.

As the blade lanced toward me, I spun away, shouldering through one of the stall doors. He tried to come in after me. I grabbed hold of the door and slammed it on him, catching his arm for a second. He pulled free—and before he could force his way in, I slammed the door shut and shot the bolt.

This had to be fast—lightning fast. The door was light, the lock was flimsy. He would break through in an instant.

I didn't wait for him. I dropped to the floor. I ducked under the gap between the stalls.

There was an enormous crash as the knife-man kicked his way into the locked stall—the one I'd just left.

I flew out the door of the other stall, and in a split second I was behind him.

The killer already realized he'd been tricked. He was starting to turn from the empty stall, to turn toward me.

Too bad, brother, one mistake is all you get. I punched

him fast and hard in the nose. His head flew back, blood bursting from his nostrils. I didn't let him recover. I grabbed hold of his wrist—the wrist of his knife hand—so he couldn't cut me. With my other hand, I grabbed his hair and bent him forward.

I dragged him out of the stall, turning my body to give me momentum. I slammed him face-first into the hard edge of the sink.

His knees buckled and he crumpled to the floor, unconscious.

I stood over him, gasping for breath, amazed that I was still alive.

CHAPTER TWO

Surrounded

I knelt down beside the fallen killer.

He didn't move. His upper lip was all smashed up and there was dark blood smearing his mouth. His mouth was open and I could see the blood staining his teeth too.

I began to search his clothes. I knew I had to hurry. Someone could come into the bathroom at any moment and see me kneeling over his body. They would call for help and then I'd have the police after me again.

Quickly, I went through the pockets of his windbreaker first. They were empty. Then, one by one, I went through the pockets of his jeans. In the left front pocket I found a single key on a chain. The key was unmarked, but the chain said, "Harley-Davidson Motorcycles." I slipped the key into my pocket. I figured that would slow the guy down at least.

I went on searching. In his right front pocket I found a silver money clip with about two hundred dollars in it. Yes, I know the Ten Commandments and yes, I know you're not supposed to steal. But this didn't feel like stealing. The guy was a killer, after all—my killer, if he'd had his way. I figured he owed me at least this much. I stuffed the cash into the same pocket as the key.

Just then, the killer groaned and shifted. I tensed, watching him. His hand lifted from the floor and groped weakly at the air. His eyelids fluttered. His bloody mouth moved, his lips parting. He was starting to come around.

I was running out of time. I had to get out of here.

I scooped up the knife from the floor. I slipped the brutal blade under my belt so that it went into my pocket. I pulled down my fleece so that it hid the handle. That's when I noticed the blood on my hands. It was the killer's blood, plus some of my own from my bruised knuckles. I turned on the faucet, let the cold water run over my fingers. It stung like crazy, but I forced myself to keep my hands there as the blood washed off. I watched as the red streaks stained the water and swirled with it down the drain.

Finally, I splashed cold water on my face again, just as I had before the killer came in. Just as I had then, I pulled a couple of paper towels out of the dispenser and dried myself off quickly.

And just as I had before, I looked into the mirror. I looked at my own reflection.

I was pale now. My cheeks were a weird gray, the color of concrete, only with spots here and there of frantic red. A line of sweat ran down my temple.

But my eyes were determined.

The killer gave another low groan. He shifted on the floor as he continued to wake up.

I swiped the line of sweat off my face. It was time to go.

I moved to the door and pushed through. I walked down the little hallway that led into the main part of the library's second floor.

It was pretty much your usual library: one expansive room filled with shelves of books. There were some long reading tables in front of the shelves. There were people sitting at the tables, poring over open books and writing in notebooks. There was an information desk to my right with a librarian sitting on a high stool behind it. The walls were all made of steel-framed glass, big windows looking out at the sky and the buildings of downtown Whitney and Main Street below.

It seemed strange to me that everything should be normal here, everything quiet and peaceful, the way a library ought to be. I thought the whole room would've heard me fighting with the killer in the bathroom. But in fact, the fight had happened with hardly a sound. No one suspected.

I glanced at the exits. There were two of them. There was one staircase down to the main floor on my left and another to my right, just beside the information desk. I was about to head for the staircase on my left.

But I stopped before I even took a step.

There was a man loitering there. A small, wiry, olive-skinned man with a thin mustache. He was wearing khaki slacks and a brown jacket. He was leaning against a shelf, idly turning the pages of a dictionary.

I turned to the other stairway. I saw another man—a man sitting at a reading desk near the head of the stairs. He was a short guy, too, but thick and muscular and mean-looking. He had a block-shaped head with short hair and rough skin on his cheeks. He was staring down at a news-paper that lay open on the desk in front of him.

I looked back at the mustache-man near the left stair-case. Back at the block-headed man to my right.

They were Homelanders. I knew it the moment I saw them.

They had both exits blocked. I was surrounded.

CHAPTER THREE

All I Know

My name is Charlie West. Until a year ago, I was a pretty
ordinary kid. I was seventeen. I lived in a house in Spring
Hill with my mom and dad and my annoying older sister,
Amy. I went to high school during the week. I went to
church on Sunday. My secret ambition was to join the air
force and become a fighter pilot, which I thought would
be a cool way to serve my country.

I wasn't the most popular kid in school, but I wasn't an
untouchable or anything either. I had some good friends:
Josh Lerner, who was kind of a geek, and Rick Donnelly

and Kevin "Miler" Miles, who were both athletes. I was a pretty decent athlete myself. My sport was karate. I was good at it. I had earned my black belt.

What else do you need to know? There was a girl. Beth Summers. I liked her. A lot. A guy I knew named Alex Hauser liked her too. He used to be my best friend, but he'd gotten into some bad stuff after his parents got divorced. We'd kind of grown apart and I guess you could say we'd become rivals for Beth's affection.

Anyway, that was my life, my ordinary Spring Hill kid life.

Then one day I went to bed and when I woke up, that life was gone. Suddenly, somehow, it was a year later—a whole year had disappeared just like that and I couldn't remember any of it. Suddenly, somehow, I was in the clutches of a group of madmen who called themselves the Homelanders. They were terrorists, foreign Islamists, out to destroy America, recruiting Americans to help them, people who could move around the country more easily than they could without arousing suspicion.

They told me I was one of them, a terrorist myself. But I didn't believe it. I couldn't believe it. I mean, I love this country. You're free here to do and think what you want, to be whatever you can be. I'd never do anything to hurt America.

I guess the Homelanders must've figured that out because they tried to kill me. I escaped and called the police. Which you'd think was a good idea, right? As it turned out: no. As it turned out, the police were after me too. Somehow, during this year—this year I couldn't remember—I had become a wanted man. I'd been put on trial and convicted of murdering Alex Hauser, my former best friend.

So now, not only were the Homelanders trying to kill me, but the police, led by this very angry detective named Rose, were trying to catch me and throw me into prison.

There was no one I could turn to. My parents had moved away and I didn't know where to find them. Nobody believed me about the Homelanders—or if they did, they thought I was one of them. And how could I prove I wasn't, when I didn't remember anything?

Sometimes, to be honest, I wasn't even sure myself.

And that's where things stood. The situation was bad—crazy bad. Some days, it almost seemed impossible. But I'd promised God and I'd promised myself that, no matter what, I would never give in.

CHAPTER FOUR
The Killer in Question

But now here I was, trapped in the library, both exits blocked. I felt fear closing around my throat like cold fingers. I figured there were probably more of these Homelander thugs downstairs, even more of them outside watching the doors. If I tried to leave, they would wait till I got outside and kill me. If I screamed for help, they would kill me right here. There was no way out.

Now the two men saw me. Mustache-Man cast a glance over at Blockhead, and Blockhead glanced back. Obviously, they'd been waiting here, waiting for the blond killer to finish me off in the bathroom. I guess they weren't very happy to see me come out alive. Well, too bad for them.

I had to think of something. I had to figure out a way to get past them. They were staying cool, staying at their posts by the stairs. They didn't want any open violence. They didn't want to cause any trouble in public if they could help it. They preferred waiting for me to go outside.

I thought maybe I could use that to my advantage somehow . . .

I started moving. I walked to the information desk. I walked casually, as if everything was fine.

The librarian was a sweet-faced older lady. As I approached her, she looked up, blinking at me vaguely through the lenses of her enormous glasses.

The block-headed man sitting at the desk kept his eye on me. He was tense. His hand hovered inside his jacket. I was pretty sure he had a gun in there. I was pretty sure if I asked the librarian for help, he would pull the gun out and start shooting.

So I didn't ask her for help. Instead, I spoke in a clear, calm voice, friendly and relaxed, as if I didn't even know Blockhead and Mustache-Man were watching.

"Excuse me, ma'am," I said pleasantly.

She was a small woman, barely five feet tall. She looked sort of bulky and shapeless in a dark flowery blouse. Her hair was short and dyed a kind of silvery blonde. Her wrinkled features were kindly but distant, abstracted, as if she were far away inside her own mind.

"Yes?" she said, in a quiet, librarian sort of voice. "Can I help you?"

I reached into the inner pocket of my fleece. I brought out the papers I had there. I chose one quickly from the pile. I handed it to her.

"Could you tell me if you have any books about this case?" I said. "I couldn't find any in the computer."

Out of the corner of my eye, I saw the blockhead cast a quick look across the room at Mustache-Man. He wasn't sure what to do, whether to make a move or not, pull his gun or not.

That's exactly what I was counting on.

The librarian took the paper from me. She peered down at it through her glasses. It was a printout of a front-page news story from the *Whitney County Register*. "Escaped Killer Thought to Have Joined Terrorist Gang," the headline read.

There was a big picture of my face in the center of the story. I was the killer in question.

The librarian blinked down at the page for a moment. Then she lifted her eyes to me.

"Let me see if I can . . ." she began to say.

Then she stopped. She saw me. She recognized my face. How could she miss it, looking at my picture like that, then looking up at me? I saw the blood drain out of her cheeks. Her parted lips began to quiver. Her eyes shifted frantically as she tried to figure out what to do.

"Would you . . . ?" she stammered. "Would you excuse me for just one moment please? I'll—I'll check on this for you. I think we may have something at one of our other branches. I'll have to give them a call and ask them. All right?"

"Sure," I said as easily as I could. "I'll just wait here."

Quickly, the librarian turned away and went through a door behind her. It led to a small office behind a large pane of glass. I could see her through the window as she moved to the office desk. She picked up the phone there. She pressed the buttons. As she waited, she glanced at the page in her hand again and then looked up at me through the glass. She forced a smile at me. I forced a smile back.

I didn't think she was really calling another branch of the library. I was pretty sure she was calling the police.

She was telling them to come and arrest me, the dangerous fugitive in her library.

At least, I hoped that's what she was doing. It was the only chance I had.

Now—as Blockhead and Mustache-Man watched me tensely—I started moving again. I walked away from the desk. Casually, I strolled across the room to the windows. I looked out through the glass at the street below, trying to see how bad the situation was.

It was worse than I thought.

The season was late autumn. The time was early evening. Dusk was falling. The office buildings of Whitney's downtown were slowly turning to silhouettes against the darkening sky. The grassy triangle of the little park across the street was disappearing into shadow beneath the naked branches of its spreading oak trees. Cars went by— not a lot, but a steady stream of them. Their white headlights flared as they approached. Their red taillights faded into the distance as they drove away.

And I could see them: the Homelanders. Waiting for me. Two hulking shadows in the park under the trees. Two more at the near corner. Two more at the far corner. Who knows how many others? Standing there. Ready. Too many to fight. Too many to get past.

My eyes shifted. I looked down at the street. There were lines of cars parked along both curbs. I moved my gaze over them slowly. I was looking for a motorcycle. I was looking for the Harley-Davidson that fit the key—the blond killer's key that was now in my pocket. I had only driven a motorcycle once before in my life. The older brother of a friend of mine had let me try it. I had a natural feel for it and by the time I'd driven it a short distance, I was maneuvering the big machine pretty well. I thought if I could somehow get past all those thugs in the shadows, if I could get to the Harley fast, get on it fast—well, maybe then I could use it to escape.

My eyes continued moving over the line of cars. My breath caught. I felt a small spark of excitement and hope. I had spotted the motorcycle.

Then, the very next moment, the spark of hope died. I felt my stomach go sour.

There were two of them. Two motorcycles. One was parked at the near curb, down by the corner to my left. One was parked on the other curb, almost directly across the street from the library entrance and in front of the park. In the gathering darkness, I couldn't tell whether one or both of them were Harleys that might match my key.

I might—might just—be able to make a mad dash and reach one of the bikes. But how could I tell which bike to choose, which one the key fit?

"Don't even think about it. You'll never make it."

CHAPTER FIVE

No Way Out

It was as if my own thought had been spoken out loud—spoken in a low, mocking, foreign voice.

I turned and felt a shock as I saw that the olive-skinned Mustache-Man had sidled up beside me. He was so close that, when he spoke again, I felt his hot breath on my face.

"Every way is blocked. Every avenue is covered. If you come with us quietly, perhaps we may be able to work something out."

Right, I thought. *Work something out. Like what? A bullet to the brain and a shallow grave?*

I was scared—really scared. But I managed to give him a hard stare. "Thanks anyway," I said.

The man's lip curled in what was half a smile, half a sneer. "You were the one who chose to betray us, West. You'll only make it worse for yourself if you draw things out."

He lifted his chin. I followed the gesture and turned. The other guy, the blockhead, was standing at my other shoulder. He held his jacket open a little and gave me a peek at the deadly-looking automatic pistol hidden in a shoulder holster underneath.

"Here's your choice, my friend," said Mustache-Man. "You can leave with us now or we're going to shoot you right here. We're going to shoot you and anyone else who tries to get in our way. It could be a very bloody business."

What could I say? I was sure they would do it. Who knew how many innocent people they would kill if I didn't go with them? For a moment, I hesitated, silent, desperately listening. Desperately hoping to hear sirens approaching. The cops might catch me, might take me to prison, but at least they wouldn't kill me. Where were they? Where were the sirens?

There was nothing. Not a sound. Maybe I was wrong. Maybe the librarian hadn't called the police after all.

"You will please turn around now," said Mustache-Man quietly.

I turned around—and there, standing right in front of me, was the blond killer from the bathroom. He'd wiped his face, but I could still see blood on his upper lip. I could see the rage in his eyes too. He couldn't wait to get me outside and get his revenge.

He reached out and lifted my fleece, exposing the knife in my belt—his knife. Quickly, he yanked the knife free and slipped it into his windbreaker.

"You will please to move to the stairs," said Mustache-Man.

"Don't try anything, West," said the blond killer with fiery eyes.

I hesitated one more second. Listening for those police sirens. Nothing.

"To the stairs," said Mustache-Man. "Now."

What could I do?

They surrounded me, Blockhead on one side, Mustache-Man on the other, Blond Killer at my back. They marched me across the room.

A sense of helplessness rose in me. Helplessness and growing panic. I couldn't fight them or innocent people would get shot. But once they got me out of the library, once they got me out on the street in the gathering darkness, it would be over. All those shadows—all those thugs out there—they'd have me bundled into a car in a second. They would take me away and that would be the end of it, the end of me. No one would even know what had happened.

The three thugs herded me steadily across the room, keeping me hemmed in. They crossed in front of the information desk, heading for the staircase on the right.

I turned to glance at the desk. The sweet-faced librarian was just now coming out of her office. She stopped in her tracks and stared at me as I went walking past with the three men. Had she called the police to tell them she had spotted a fugitive? Were they coming? There was no way I could know for sure.

The men hustled me past her quickly. She watched us go by. She didn't try to stop me. She didn't say anything. Neither did I.

Then we were at the stairs. The thugs escorted me down. It was all happening very fast. There was no time to resist, no time even to think. Another moment and we were on the ground floor. There was the checkout desk right ahead of us, a small line of people with books moving slowly past two more librarians. Beyond that, there was a set of glass doors, the front doors leading to the street.

Beyond those, the Homelanders were waiting.

Mustache-Man's hand tightened on my arm. He knew this was the time, this was my last chance to make a break for it. He wasn't going to let it happen.

My eyes went this way and that, frantically. Still no sirens, still no sign of the police.

There were only a few steps left before we were outside, lost in the twilight. Mustache-Man kept his grip on me while, with his other hand, he reached out to push the library door open.

I didn't try to run. I didn't have the nerve. I didn't want to get shot and I didn't want anyone else to get shot either. I had to wait, had to hope the librarian had called the cops, that they were on their way, that they would get here on time.

Mustache-Man opened the door. He went out first, drawing me after him into the cold night air. The blockhead and the blond killer were right behind us.

Now we were outside, standing on the library's top step with three more steps leading down from the door to the street. I had a sense that the shadows all around me—the Homelanders who had been waiting for us—were even now converging on us, closing in to make sure I didn't get away.

The blond killer came around from behind me and went down the stairs ahead of us. He moved to a big dark car parked underneath a sidewalk plane tree. He opened the car's rear door—like a chauffeur waiting for his passenger. Only he was waiting for me and my two escorts. Waiting for them to put me in the dark car so they could drive me away to my place of execution.

A light seemed to go out inside me, the light of hope. I had been wrong. The librarian hadn't recognized me after all. She hadn't called the police. There was no help coming, no way I could escape.

Mustache-Man and Blockhead started to hustle me down the stairs toward the open door of the dark car.

And just then, the sirens and lights exploded all around us.

CHAPTER SIX

Two Motorcycles

The police had approached the library quietly, trying not to scare me off. But now they saw me making my escape and they charged in to stop me. The blaring sirens and flashing lights went off like bombs. Four patrol cars came swooping in toward the library, two screeching around the corner from the left, two more from the right.

Mustache-Man, Blockhead, and I had just reached the last stair and were about to step down onto the sidewalk. The blond killer was holding the door of the dark car open only a few yards away. Other men, other thugs, were lurking in the shadows at the edges of my vision, lurking all around us in the deepening dusk.

But when the air suddenly filled with the screaming sirens, when the oncoming night suddenly burned red and blue with the cruisers' lights, everyone froze in place, startled. Mustache-Man. Blockhead. Blond Killer. The shadows all around. Everyone froze.

Everyone but me.

I was the only one who'd been expecting it—hoping for it. I was the only one who was ready to move.

At the first siren's wail, I yanked my arm free of Mustache-Man's grip. He tried to react. He started to turn. A stiletto—a long, thin knife—suddenly flashed in his hand in the light of the streetlamp.

But he wasn't quick enough. I brought my fist down like a hammer on the bridge of his nose. Blood sprayed from his nostrils as his head flew back. In the same movement, with the same arm, I sent my elbow driving back, smashing it into Blockhead's teeth.

The thugs fell away from me. Blockhead stumbled off the bottom step and spilled to the pavement.

That was all the room I needed. I leapt forward and ran—not toward the dark car, but toward another car parked behind it. I threw myself at the hood, hit the top of it, and rolled. I dropped off the other side, landing on my feet in the middle of the street.

Blinded by the headlights of the onrushing cop cars, I stumbled forward but managed to keep my balance, to keep moving. In less than a second, I was rushing for the far curb, rushing for the motorcycle I'd seen from the window, the one parked just across from the entrance, just in front of the grassy park.

I didn't know if it was the right motorcycle, the one the key in my pocket would fit. There was still that other one parked farther down the street. But this one was closer. This was the only one I could get to before the police cars reached the front of the library.

I had no choice. I had to take the chance.

What happened next took only an instant, but that instant seemed to go on forever. Everything around me was noise and light and confusion. The discordant screams of the sirens, like cries from a jungle where the animals have all gone insane. The white glare of the headlights stampeding toward me. The whirl of the red and blue flashers bouncing off the trees and the cars and the sidewalks and the dark of evening with a sort of crazy gaiety. Even as I ran through that onrushing chaos, I glanced back over my shoulder. And yes, I saw the hulking shadows of the Homelanders. I saw them hurrying away, slipping off into the deeper shadows, escaping the police. None of them paused to shout after me. None of them drew a gun and took aim. None of them dared. The police were just too close, screaming closer and closer with every moment. There was nothing the Homelanders could do but run for it and hope to find me again another time.

So now—for me—there were just the police. Just, that is, the threat of being arrested again, of being sent back to prison for murder, put in a cell for twenty-five years.

I faced forward and ran with all the speed I had in me.

Two more steps—two, then three—and I was there, at the motorcycle. I saw the orange-and-white logo: it was a Harley at least. But was it the right one? With one hand I was reaching out for the handlebars. My other hand was in my pocket, my fingers on the key I'd taken from the blond killer in the bathroom. I pulled the key from my pocket even as I grabbed the handlebar and threw my leg over the cycle's seat.

In the same instant, I heard the hoarse screech of tires as the police hit their brakes. The cruisers jolted to a halt right beside me, to the left and right of me, blocking the street off in both directions.

I jammed the key into the bike's ignition.

The sirens stopped. I heard the cruiser doors thumping open. I heard shouts in the night.

"Hold it, West!"

"Hold it right there!"

"Freeze!"

For one second, I looked up, looked around me. I saw the faces of policemen going blood-red and night-black as the flashers played over them. I saw their figures poised and tense, their arms at their holsters—and then lifting, bringing up their guns, bringing them to bear on me.

Did I have the right motorcycle? Did I have the right one?

I turned the key.

CHAPTER SEVEN

Harley

The Harley shuddered as the engine roared to life. A prayer of thanks leapt from my heart to heaven. Above the throaty grumble, through the whirl of colored lights, I heard the police still shouting.

"Get off it, West!"

"Stand down!"

"Don't try it!"

All together, I kicked the bike's stand away with my heel, twisted the transmission into gear, twisted the throttle, and wrenched the handlebars, turning the front wheel sharply.

"Stop!"

The bike leapt forward. It jumped the curb, jumped up on the sidewalk. I poured on the gas and roared off into the park, over the grass and into the dark shadows beneath the overhanging oaks.

I don't know if any of the policemen shot at me. I'd have been pretty hard to hit, moving that fast through the darkness of the little square. For what seemed like a long time—a long, mad, terrifying time—I was only aware of the rumble of the bike and the nauseating thrill of the speed and the movement of the air washing over my face as I bounced and sped across the lawn.

Then, in the glow of a streetlamp, I saw pavement. The white pavement of the walkway through the square. I twisted the wheel and headed for it.

The bike was unsteady on the soft ground, but the minute it hit the pavement, it seemed to right itself and gain traction. It leapt forward, dashing over the walkway, racing even faster than it had before.

I looked up, looked ahead. There were dark shadows under another row of oaks at the edge of the square. Then, just beyond that, there was a streetlamp's glow and the far sidewalk—and the far street, the next street over, where I could see the headlights of cars whisking past in the early evening.

I turned the bike again and headed for the sidewalk. I felt the tires grow unsteady under me as they left the pavement and hit the grass. The lacework shadows of bare branches fell over me. The thick trunks of the oaks loomed in front of me, the light of the sidewalk street-lamps visible in between. I headed for one of the gaps between trees, aiming to break out onto the sidewalk, to leap off into the street and make a getaway.

The gap of light grew larger as the bike raced toward it unsteadily. With the soft earth gripping at the tires, I could feel the machine trying to wrench itself out of my control. I fought hard to aim the bike at the light between the trees.

Then, suddenly, a silhouette blocked the way. It was a woman. A pedestrian walking along the sidewalk. She was just passing by, blocking the space between the tree trunks. She didn't see me heading straight toward her.

And I was—I was heading straight toward her at high speed, with no room to maneuver. If I tried to get around her—tried to turn the bike to the left or the right—I was sure to smash into one of the tree trunks. If I tried to avoid the trees—tried to swerve out of the way—I would lose control of the bike in the grass and go down—and go down hard.

I had about three more seconds before I hit her, three seconds to decide. There was no way out of it. I had to turn the bike. I wasn't going to crash into an innocent person. I had to hit the tree or fall.

I gripped the handlebars, ready to try the turn.

And just then she heard me, heard the roar of the approaching engine. She glanced my way. Saw the bike shooting toward her.

I couldn't hear her scream over the motorcycle noise, but I'm pretty sure she did. I could tell by the way she threw her hands up. By the way her head went back. I could even see her eyes widen in shock and her mouth open in the light of the streetlamp. In her fear, she froze, smack in my path. Then, instinctively, she dodged backward.

That did it. That was all I needed. Her movement opened a little space between her and the tree to the right. The bike's tires wobbled dangerously as I wrestled them around to point in the direction of that narrow gap.

Then I burst through. Out between the trees. Out of the small park's shadows. Out onto the sidewalk and into the glow of the streetlamps.

And a wall of parked cars loomed in front of me.

I hit the brakes. The bike's spinning tires seized. The bike angled sideways under me. It skidded past the startled pedestrian, slid sideways across the sidewalk, carrying me helplessly toward the parked cars.

I thumped against the side of a Toyota, pinching my leg between the car door and the bike. The motorcycle had nearly stopped by that time and though the impact was hard enough to send a shock of pain through me, it wasn't hard enough to do any real damage.

The next second, I had the bike righted. I gave it gas again. I felt it dart forward under me, racing a little way along the sidewalk until I spotted an opening between parked cars.

The bike made the gap. I bounced hard over the curb. I rolled out into the street, already gathering speed again.

There was a wild screaming blare: a car horn. A huge sedan was barreling toward me, its headlights like a pair of eyes jacked wide in fear.

I cried out as I wrenched the bike's handlebars. The tires of the onrushing sedan screeched as the car swerved in the opposite direction. We passed each other by inches, so close I felt the side of the car flick at the cloth of my jeans.

Then the bike turned, shot forward. I was heading

down the street, the park to the right of me, a row of shops to my left. Up ahead, I saw a corner, a traffic light. A van was stopped on the cross street, the driver waiting for the light to change. The light was green facing me—then it was yellow. I was going to have to be quick if I wanted to make it through.

I heard the sirens start again. Even with the roar of the motorcycle enveloping me, there was no mistaking that sound. I glanced to the side and saw the red and blue flashers through the trees, saw them moving on the other side of the park as the police cars started up again.

The traffic light turned red. The van started moving. I didn't slow down. I raced into the intersection. The van loomed to my left. I heard its tires screech. Then I was past it. The driver shouted curses behind me.

I looked back over my shoulder. Before the van could even start up again, the police cars were at the corner, coming around it, sirens screaming.

I gave the motorcycle gas and raced on, with the police right behind me.

And somewhere, deep inside me, there was this little voice, saying, *Maybe you should stop. Maybe you should give yourself up. Maybe the police are right.*

Maybe you're the bad guy.

CHAPTER EIGHT
The Truth You Live

In quiet moments there were things that came back to me sometimes—things from my life before this nightmare started. I thought a lot about my karate teacher, for instance: Sensei Mike.

Sensei Mike was just about the coolest guy I ever met. He'd been in the army for a long time and had fought the Islamic extremists in both Afghanistan and Iraq. He even got a medal from the president of the United States because he once helped hold off an attack by a hundred bad guys with a .50-caliber gun mounted on an armored truck. He never talked about that, but I looked it up on the Internet and found out what happened. He'd been wounded in the fight and had to come home and have a piece of titanium put in his leg. He never talked about that either.

But he did talk about a lot of other things. About karate mostly, of course. How to fight—and how to avoid a fight if there was any possible way you could. How to control your emotions and your body. How to harness your fears and transform your nervousness into energy and focus. He talked a lot about focus, about paying attention—not just to karate but to everything, to the people you loved and the people who needed you, and just to everything you were trying to accomplish, to life in general.

"Here's the deal, chucklehead," he told me once. "God wants you to have a big, full, terrific life. And you can't have that kind of life unless you're paying attention."

I guess Mike was somewhere in his thirties. He was about my height, but with broader shoulders. He had this thick, black hair that he was very proud of. He always kept it neatly combed, even when he was working out. He had this big drooping mustache that he was proud of too. If you looked carefully, behind the mustache and into his eyes, you could usually see him smiling, as if he found everything kind of funny. After everything he'd been through, I don't think there was really very much in life that Mike took seriously. Only a few things. Only the things that really mattered.

Anyway, this one time, something happened in the dojo . . . Well, it all ended up in the dojo, but it started before that. It started that morning in history class with my teacher Mr. Sherman.

I had Mr. Sherman in history two years running. He was a trim, fit, youthful-looking guy, handsome in a sort of bland way with a friendly smile and intelligent eyes. I never thought he was a bad person or anything, but, to be honest, I did think he was kind of a doofus. My problem with him—the thing you could say sort of constituted his doofy-os-itude—was that he fancied himself some kind of big-time radical. He was always trying to get us to "question our assumptions." And look, there's nothing wrong with that as a general sort of thing. It's just that Mr. Sherman sort of took it to the Crazy Place, if you know what I mean.

See, Mr. Sherman's point of view was that nothing was really good or bad, it was just a matter of how you thought about it. Now that didn't make any sense to me, but I have to admit I sometimes found it hard to argue with him.

That's what happened this one morning in class. We'd been having a discussion about current events. Mr. Sherman was sitting on the edge of his desk, tossing one of the whiteboard markers in the air and catching it. "The problem with this country," he was saying, "is that too many people believe blindly in absolute morality, absolute truth. Our country was founded on absolutes: truths that are supposedly 'self-evident.' And because we believe our truths are absolute and self-evident, we're only too quick to hate other people and impose our truths on them. Absolutism is the meat of tyrants. Real morality is always changing. It depends on your situation and your cultural tradition."

Now there were so many things about this statement that I thought were false, they kind of got jammed up in my brain as they tried to get to my mouth. For one thing, there are a lot of countries in the world that hate other people and attack other countries without reason, or that try to force even their own citizens to believe things whether they want to or not. America never does that. But before I could even get to that point, I blurted out:

"Wait a minute. You're talking about the Declaration of Independence, right? The only truths it holds to be 'self-evident' are that all men are created equal. And that their Creator gave them the rights to life, liberty, and the pursuit of happiness."

"Ah, I knew we'd hear from Charlie on this one," said Mr. Sherman, looking around at the rest of the class. "Charlie is a True Believer. I can always count on him to follow blindly along with the crowd. The All-American Zombie." He put his hands out in front of him like a zombie and let his mouth hang open. "Night of the Living Charlie."

This was another thing that always annoyed me about Mr. Sherman. When you argued with him, he didn't exactly use facts and logic. He just tried to make fun of you and change the subject and tangle you up with words so you looked bad or the class laughed at you and you got flustered and couldn't make your point. And another thing that annoyed me was that a lot of times it worked.

I glanced around at the rest of the students. They were all laughing at Mr. Sherman's zombie routine. Even Rick Donnelly, one of my best friends, was laughing over at his desk near the window. I knew Rick agreed with me about Mr. Sherman. He thought this was a great country and even wanted to go into politics when he grew up. But he was the kind of guy who never argued with teachers, who was always trying to please them and say what they wanted to hear so he would get good grades. Maybe that's how you get to be a politician.

"So what part of the Declaration don't you agree with?" I asked Mr. Sherman.

Sherman stopped waving his arms around. He smiled. "Ah, my zombielike friend, that's exactly the wrong question. The question is: What part of it can you prove to be true? Prove that we're created equal. We don't look equal to me."

"That's not what it means. It means that we're created with equal rights."

"Prove it, Charlie. You can't. It's just something Americans have come to believe, that's all. Other people believe other things. You can't even prove that we were created, that we have a Creator in the first place. It's just something you were told and so you believe it. Go on, Zombie Guy—prove it."

I opened my mouth to answer, but I couldn't think what to say. I didn't know exactly how you would prove something like that. Sherman made the class laugh at me again by opening his mouth and making stuttering sounds to imitate my confusion: "Uh, uh, uh!"

Then the bell rang. That was the end of class.

"All right, that's it," said Sherman, "unless you guys

want to stay behind and listen to Charlie sing the national anthem."

That made everyone laugh again. And they were still laughing as they filed out of the room.

So I guess Sherman won that argument or at least got the last laugh. And yeah, it bothered me. I felt bad that the kids laughed, and I felt especially bad that I hadn't been able to come up with a good argument for what I was trying to say. It made me angry—because I knew I was right and he was wrong.

I guess I was still a little angry when I went to the dojo that afternoon for my karate lesson.

Here's what happened. There was this other kid, Peter Williams. He was taking a lesson that day too. Sensei Mike decided to have us do some *kumite*. Kumite is sparring without protective gear, without soft gloves and helmets and shin pads and everything. In kumite, you just dress in your *gi*—your karate outfit—and you use your bare hands and feet with your head and body unprotected.

So, of course, with kumite, you have to be extra careful. You strike with the open hand and not the fist, and you make sure to pull all your strikes and kicks so no one gets hurt. It's an exercise meant to teach you control—and also to teach you not to be afraid of getting hit from time to time.

Sensei Mike told us to begin and Peter and I started to circle around each other, looking for an opening, ready to fight. Now, Peter went to a different high school than I did and I didn't know him very well, but he always seemed like a good enough guy. He was smaller than I was, but wiry, muscular, and very fast. He had good high kicks that could catch you on the shoulder or even the head if you weren't careful. And he was hard to hit because he knew how to dance around and dodge.

I knew Peter liked to stay away from you and then suddenly dart in for a strike. That way he could use his speed to his advantage. My strategy against him was to stay on defense: stay back, stay focused, keep a good eye on him, and try to figure out when he was about to make his rush. That way, I could usually stop his attack and come back at him with a counterattack of my own.

The first time Peter rushed me, this strategy worked really well. Peter dashed at me across the carpeted dojo floor and launched a front ball kick at my stomach. I managed to dodge out of the way, but he followed up quickly with a slap at my head. I blocked the slap with my arm and then sent a sort of backhanded slap of my own into his belly. Again, we were unprotected, so we only used our open hands and were careful not to hit too hard.

Peter retreated, circling and dancing too far away for me to reach, looking for another opening into which he could rush again. I waited him out. I was paying close attention. I was ready for his rush. But none of that mattered. He was just too quick this time, too good. He rushed in with a fake, pretending to strike low. Then he came up fast at my head. I fell for it. I blocked him low and he came in over the top of the block and landed a good solid slap to the side of my forehead.

Peter kept full control of his strike. He didn't hurt me or anything, so there was nothing wrong with it. If you spar, sometimes you get hit, that's just the way it is. As Sensei Mike always told us, "You gotta lose to learn."

But there was something wrong with what happened next. There was something very wrong about it.

I felt a flash of anger go through me. Even though he hadn't injured me, I didn't like getting fooled and I didn't like getting hit. It hurt my pride. And I guess the thing is, too, I was already angry when I came to the dojo. I was angry because of what happened in Sherman's class. Having Peter outfight me like that just set the anger off.

Before I even had a chance to think, I snapped back

at him. I ducked under his guard and shot my forearm into his midsection. It landed with more force than I meant—a lot more. I heard him say, "Oof," as the air rushed out of him. I should have pulled back then, but it was too late to stop. I was already moving, already bringing the back of my hand up toward his face. It was an openhanded strike and all that, but my knuckles cracked against Peter's chin. His head flew back and he stumbled away from me, dazed.

I didn't stop then either. I was still angry. I charged right after him, ready to deliver another series of strikes to his gut and to his face. I took—I don't know—maybe half a step.

And then, Sensei Mike came between us.

He moved so quickly I had no time to react. In one simultaneous combination, he grabbed my arm, hit me in the chest with his palm, and used his foot to sweep my leg out from under me. I went down hard, my back landing on the carpet with a bone-shaking *thud*. Mike's move took me by such surprise that I just barely managed to slap the floor, breaking my fall. Even so, the air was knocked out of me. I lay there for a moment, winded.

Mike turned his back on me and went to Peter.

"You okay, buddy?" he asked him.

Peter rubbed his chin and gave the sensei a lopsided smile. "Oh yeah. I'm fine. It's nothing."

"Good man."

I climbed slowly to my feet. Mike didn't say anything to me. He didn't have to. I already felt terrible. What a stupid thing to do.

"Hey, Peter, I am really sorry, man," I said. "I totally lost control. Way, way out of line. No excuse. I'm just sorry."

Peter shrugged. He smiled. "No problem, bro. Heat of battle. It happens."

I guess that was true enough. It was the heat of battle, and these things do happen. But that still didn't make it all right. When you train with someone, you're on the same team, even when you're fighting. The idea isn't to hurt him, it's to help him learn by forcing him to compete and get better. I felt really bad about what I'd done. But I felt even worse—a lot worse—about what I would have done—what I meant to do—if Mike hadn't stopped me.

We continued our lesson, even doing a little more kumite before we moved on to practicing *katas*. Sensei Mike didn't say anything more about my slipup. He didn't yell at me or lecture me or anything like that. I guess he could see how bad I felt about it already.

After the lesson, though, after Peter had left and I had changed back into my street clothes, I came out of the changing room. I was carrying my karate bag and kind of dragging my feet, keeping my head down, still feeling bad.

I came out of the dojo and into the little foyer. I stopped by the open door of Mike's office. He was sitting in the swivel chair behind his gunmetal-gray desk. He was looking over something on his computer.

"Hey, Mike, I really am sorry about the kumite," I told him.

He glanced up. "Yeah, I heard you the first time. You apologized like a man and Pete forgave you. You don't have to torture yourself about it. Like he said, it was the heat of battle. It's not like you really hurt him or anything."

"I know," I said. And then I said, "But I would've. I'd have kept going after him, if you hadn't stopped me."

Mike shrugged. "That's what I'm here for, chuckle-head."

"Yeah, but you won't always be there."

He tilted back in his chair, put his feet up on the desk and his hands behind his head. He laughed and his eyes kind of laughed with him. "Sure I will. I'm your teacher. I'm in your head, double-ugly. You'll never get rid of me. That's why you have to be careful who you learn from."

I couldn't tell whether he was kidding around or not. It was like that a lot with Mike. He would say something that sounded serious, but there'd still be that laughter hiding under the 'stache.

"Why don't you tell me what's biting your butt, any-way?" he said now. "What got you all angry today? It wasn't Peter, that's for sure. I saw there was something stuck in your craw the minute you started working out."

I don't know why I should've been surprised by this. It was a weird thing about Mike. He could watch you practice karate and know almost exactly what you were thinking. I'd seen him do it a dozen times.

I sighed. I figured I might as well tell him. "I have this teacher at school . . ." I said. And then I laid it all out, explaining about Mr. Sherman and what he'd said in class and how I couldn't figure out how to answer him.

When I was finished, Mike did this thing he did a lot, where he would sort of smooth his mustache down with his thumb and forefinger for a long time. That way, you couldn't see him smiling at all, though you always suspected he was.

"So let me ask you something," he said. "Do you love your mom?"

"What?"

"Your female parental unit. Your mom. You love her?"

"Yeah. Sure, I love my mom. I mean, she worries too much, but basically she's a really good mom. In fact, I love her a lot."

"Prove it."

I laughed. "I . . . I mean . . . I can't . . . I . . ."

Mike opened his mouth and went, "Uh, uh, uh," pretending to make fun of me the way Mr. Sherman had.

"All right," I said finally, "I can't prove it, but there's, like, stuff I do, you know. I mean, she knows I love her."

"Sure she does. 'Cause you treat her with respect. You try to make her proud of you. You give her a little affection when no one's looking. Maybe clean your room every fifty, hundred years or so."

"Yeah. Right. Stuff like that," I said.

"See, that's the thing, pal. There are some truths you can't prove," Mike said. "There are some truths you can only live. Most of the really important truths—like the ones in the Declaration—you take them on faith at first. But then you live them, and that's how you find out they're really true."

"Okay," I said, thinking it over. "That makes sense, I guess. But then you might make a mistake, right? You might think something's true at first and then live it and find out it's not."

"You not only might—you will. Everyone does. That's how you learn to do better. No one starts out with the answers. You figure them out as you go and you learn from the people who figured them out before you. Like I said, it matters who your teachers are."

"But then, Mr. Sherman's right, in a way: if you might be wrong sometimes—if you might be doing something wrong right now or your country might be doing something wrong—then maybe you just think you're the good guys when you're really the bad guys. I mean, how can you tell whether you're the good guys or not?"

Mike didn't answer right away. He went on stroking his 'stache a long time. Then he said, "Put it this way, chucklehead. Say you got a bunch of people and they're all chained up in a dark place, a pitch-black place, stumbling around in their chains. But there's a light far off in the distance. And one day, some of the people start talking to each other and they say, 'Hey, we're tired of living in the dark. Why don't we break these chains and head for that light?' And at first, they can't figure out how to do it. So they talk about it some more and argue about it and even fight about it. But after a while, they come up with a way to get themselves loose and they start walking. Now remember, it's still dark where they are, so they stumble a lot and take wrong turns, and they've still got some of those old chains on them, and that makes them stumble too. But they keep moving, keep trying to get the chains off, keep heading for that light, no matter what, no matter who tries to stop them. And people do try to stop them— a lot of people. Because a lot of people like to be in the dark where no one can see what they are. And a lot of people even like to be in chains and they want to put other people in chains with them. But our guys, these people we're talking about—they keep moving, some faster, some slower, still stumbling, still half blind, half chained, still arguing about the right way. But whatever happens, they keep moving toward the light."

Mike pressed his mustache down one last time and held it there, so I couldn't see whether there was a smile on his lips or not. There was a smile in his eyes, though. I could see that. His eyes were laughing.

And he said, "Who do you think the good guys are, chucklehead?"

CHAPTER NINE

Collision

Who do you think the good guys are?

That was the question. And it haunted me. It bothered me all the time. Because the policemen are the good guys, right? They're trying to protect people and arrest bad guys.

And here they were, trying to arrest me!

They thought I'd committed murder. They thought I'd killed my friend Alex. A jury had even convicted me.

And I couldn't remember any of it. I couldn't even remember Alex getting killed. So how did I know I was innocent? You see what I'm saying? How did I know if I was the good guy or the bad guy?

There was no time to think about it now. I was still racing through the night at top speed with the police on my trail. The air all around me was trembling with sirens, dancing with flashing lights. The machine underneath me was shuddering as if it were half alive. I felt that at any moment it might rear up and throw me off, pull itself out of my control and go spinning across the street. I held on as hard as I could. I fought the rattling handlebars, forcing the bike in the direction I wanted it to go. My breath was short. My heart was pounding. My stomach felt hollow with fear. Disaster—shattering injury, maybe even death—was only a single careless mistake away.

I shot down another dimly lit street of shops—and then it was gone—gone in a second. Now I was in a glaringly bright block with a lighted gas station on one side of me and a spotlit car lot on the other. Four police cars had piled into the street behind me. The lead one was close, very close, and getting closer by the second. Another block or so and it would overtake me, force me off the road or even force me down.

I looked up ahead. There was more light there. A big shopping mall with lighted signs and some fast-food joints. Before that, though, a smaller street met this one at the intersection. This smaller street ran off into shadows to my right and left. I thought if I could turn off, if I could get into those shadows, maybe I'd have some small chance of losing the cruisers behind me.

My heart seemed to rise into my throat, hammering. If I kept going straight, stayed in the light, it would only be a matter of time before they had me. But how could I make a turn, going so fast?

I wasn't sure I could. But I knew I had to try.

I brought my body low to the throbbing, stuttering bike. I said one of your basic prayers—one of those prayers that's not in the prayer book but everyone knows it anyway—something like, "Please, please, please, don't let me die!" I squinted through the onrushing wind at the intersection where the light and shadow met. I held my breath as the intersection came racing toward me.

And all of a sudden, without any warning at all, another siren started. Another set of flashing lights exploded red and blue. Another cruiser was charging toward me—this one coming toward the intersection from the side street to my right. It was moving to cut me off at the corner, to block my escape from the cops behind me and force me to stop. If it reached the corner before I did, I'd never be able to get past it, never be able to make the turn.

My whole body now felt like one enormous pulse, pounding as fast and as hard as the pulse of the engine under me. It looked certain to me that my motorcycle and the police cruiser were going to reach the corner at the same time, were going to smash into each other.

I pushed the throttle and the world sped up around me. It seemed impossible I would be able to make the turn.

I started the turn anyway. There was no oncoming traffic. The sirens had scared the other drivers off. I angled the motorcycle across the street into the other lane, hoping to slant between the approaching cruiser and the edge of the sidewalk. If I hit either one, I'd be finished.

I shot into the intersection head-on just as the cruiser shot into it from my right. We hurtled toward each other. The scream of the siren was so loud it nearly drowned out the roar of the motorcycle and the roar of my own blood in my ears. Then the scream of the cruiser's brakes joined the siren. The cop car swerved. He was trying to keep from killing me. Of course he was. He was a cop. The cops are the good guys.

As the braking cruiser turned, I slipped past its front fender on my right. I cleared the edge of the sidewalk on my left by inches. The motorcycle leaned over into the turn—and then farther over until it felt like it was practically horizontal.

Then I was around the corner. The motorcycle straightened underneath me. It gathered speed and rocketed down the smaller street. The lights of the shopping mall dropped away behind me. The shadows closed over me.

I glanced back over my shoulder. I saw the cop car still in the intersection, blocking the way. The other cruisers were rushing toward it. Their brakes were screeching now too as they tried to avoid a collision. They didn't quite make it. The first car to reach the corner clipped the tail of the cruiser that blocked the way. The car behind that one managed to swerve and avoid a rear-end crash. But the next one hit, shattering the taillight just as it got hit in turn by the car behind.

It wasn't a dangerous pileup, just a bunch of fender benders. But for a few seconds it brought all five police cars to a stop. They sat tangled together in the intersection, their flashers whirling uselessly, their sirens howling like frustrated hounds who'd lost the scent of their prey.

And I rushed on into the night.

CHAPTER TEN

Gunfire

I was in a residential section now, moving past houses and under a canopy of trees. The naked late-autumn branches interlaced above me. Through them, I could see the last light fading from the deepening blue of the sky. Fallen leaves looped up from the gutter into the air as my bike swept past them. With the sirens growing dim as they fell away behind me, it was almost quiet here for a second or two.

I slowed to take another corner. I came down another dark street of houses and turned a corner again and came down another dark street. Here the houses were small and very close together. Narrow two-story clapboards, most of them, with little porches. There was a small lawn out in front of each house, and narrow alleys between them. Most of them had lights on in the windows, sending a yellow glow out into the night.

I saw those lights and for a moment my mind drifted. I thought about the families inside those houses. They'd be sitting down to dinner with one another just now. There'd be the smell of food and the mom would be saying something to the kids like, "So what did you do at school today?" Maybe the dad would say something about what happened at work, or maybe he and the mom would talk about something, just normal stuff...

And they wouldn't know—that's what I was thinking. They wouldn't know how great things were for them. How great it was that they were all there together with plenty of food to eat and a house around them to keep them dry and warm. They wouldn't know how great it was that they were talking to one another, how lucky they were that they could all go to their rooms at the end of the day and sleep in their beds when the day was done. They wouldn't think about the fact that it could disappear, all of it, in the snap of a finger, just like that. They could wake up one morning and it could all be gone just like it was gone for me. They could find themselves out here, in the night, alone, with no food and no bed and no mom or dad or sister or brother and no friends and no one to help them. Then they would miss this dinner they were having now. They would miss it more than they thought they could ever miss anything in their lives . . .

That's what I was thinking about—when, all at once, every thought I had was blown away and the darkness and quiet all around me were blown away by a fresh howl of sirens and a sudden burst of light. Monstrous white light rushing at me headlong. Blue and red light catching the branches and the trunks of the trees.

A police car had appeared as if from nowhere, right there suddenly on the street in front of me. It was racing toward me, blocking my way, making it impossible for me to pass. I heard another siren scream and looked behind me and there was another one, another cruiser, closing in on me, cutting off my retreat.

The police cars came toward each other with me in the middle. I was blinded by the headlights. I was deafened by the noise. I was caught in the space between, caught on a little stretch of street that was getting smaller and smaller with every instant as the two cruisers rushed together.

In the seconds left to me, my eyes desperately scanned the road. There: a driveway, just to my right, the driveway to the small garage of a small, white clapboard house.

I nearly upended the bike as I turned into the drive at full speed. The sirens shrieked, the lights flashed. Now there was just the garage in front of me, a garage with a car already parked in it; no way out. Again, I looked around wildly. Now I saw the small front yard, the little brick-faced house next door—and a narrow alley between the two houses.

When I slipped out between them, the cops in the two closing cruisers found themselves rushing toward each other, toward a head-on crash. The cars braked and swerved. One bumped up onto the sidewalk, its muffler crunching into the curb as it came to a sharp stop. The other car managed to slow down enough to make the sharp turn and follow me up the driveway. He was right behind me.

I twisted the handlebars. The motorcycle hopped up onto the house's front lawn. The sudden change from pavement to soft earth made the tires go wobbly underneath me, but I couldn't slow down. I raced across the front lawn, heading for the little alley between this house and the house next door.

Behind me, the cruiser that had pulled into the driveway stopped short. I heard its doors fly open. I heard a huge, booming voice—one of the officers speaking over the car's loudspeaker: "Stop right there!"

I drove the motorcycle forward, fast but unsteady on the grass. I tried to hold on to it, tried to get control of it so I could make the turn into the narrow alley.

It was no good. I was losing control.

I hit the brakes, trying to cut my speed before the bike went over. The moment the motorcycle slowed, the soft earth seemed to grip it even harder. I felt the bike begin to slide out from under me.

It all happened with a dreamy slowness at first, and then it happened very fast. The bike tilted and tilted and I felt my body going down and down and I felt my hands losing their grip on the handlebars—and it seemed as if it was taking several hours, as if it might never come to an end.

Then—*wham*—it ended. I hit the ground and everything sped up again. I flew off the bike. I flew through the air, eerily watching the bike kick up dirt as it twisted away from me. I felt a flashing ache go through me as I hit the soft grass with my shoulder. I rolled, fast, and went on rolling. I didn't know if I was hurt. I didn't know if I'd be able to get up. But I sprang to my feet and, before I knew it, I was running.

That huge voice boomed at me again through the night. "Police! Stop right there!"

Then I was in the alley. Racing as fast as my legs would go. I brushed a garbage can and sent it spinning and clattering out in front of me. I had to leap over it to keep from tripping. I leapt and kept running.

There was a low diamond-link fence up ahead, a gate into the backyard. The breath came out of me in harsh gasps as I pumped my arms, pumped my legs, charging toward it.

Another shout: "Hold it, West! Or I'll shoot."

I was at the fence. I grabbed the top of the gate. I lifted off my feet.

A gunshot. It was like a bomb going off—unbelievably loud. There was a tearing sound. White splinters flew into the air as the bullet ripped into the corner of the house beside me, about an arm's length away.

I felt my stomach turn to water. I was so scared that if I could've stopped right then, I probably would've.

But I was already in the air, already leaping, vaulting, up over the gate, into the dark yard behind it.

I landed on my feet and ran—ran so fast I felt as if I were wearing a rocket pack. A swing set flashed by my shoulder. A sandbox flashed by my feet. A lighted window appeared in front of me. And for a moment, just a moment, I saw them: that family I'd been thinking about. The mom and dad, a son and daughter. They were sitting at a dinner table, eating and talking. I felt something lurch inside me at the sight of them. I wanted to pound on the window. I wanted to plead with them to take me in, to let me sit with them at dinner, let me have a life again away from this fear and loneliness.

But that was just a fantasy.

I saw another alley off to the right. I charged into it, and a second later I came out onto another front yard and veered off across it until I was on the street again.

I didn't slow down for an instant. There was an apartment building in front of me, and that had an alley, too, and I ran into that one, and through another yard and toward another alley.

I must've been going even faster than I thought. The police never caught up with me again. I ran and ran and ran through a broken pattern of yards and streets and alleys.

I ran until I ran out of houses. I ran until I reached the edge of town.

And then I kept running.

CHAPTER ELEVEN

Murder

There were clouds blowing by in the dark overhead, but there were great swaths of open sky. A half-moon shone, lighting my way, and I had stars enough to guide me.

I jogged down lonely country roads. When I heard cars coming, I ducked off behind the surrounding trees or dodged into an isolated driveway and hid behind a parked car.

Sometimes I heard sirens in the distance. Those were the cops, I guessed, still hunting for me. But that was back toward town, back toward Whitney. Out here, it was just me and the passing cars.

The farther I got from the little city, the easier it was to keep off the roads completely. I cut across flat farm fields harvested to the nub. I tried to lose myself in high brown grass and high brown stalks of gathered corn. Sometimes there were forests, and I'd slide in between the trees. But I couldn't go too deeply into the woods. At night, with no flashlight, it was just too dark in there, too easy to lose my way.

Once, in the middle of a great, broad space, with a vast sky of stars wheeling above me and the clouds sailing by overhead like big ships headed for faraway lands, I looked off into the distance and saw the fearful red and blue flashers of two cruisers passing on the state highway. They were heading east, toward Spring Hill. I guess it hadn't been too hard for them to figure out I was going home. I knew now they would be waiting for me, searching for me, the minute I arrived.

But I kept on. Getting tired now. My legs feeling like lead. Sometimes my head hung down and my eyes closed, as if I could sleep and walk at the same time. I was thirsty and hungry too.

I couldn't keep going. I needed a place to rest. Somewhere secluded, somewhere safe. I considered a barn I found, but the farmhouse was too close. I could see the lights in the windows, hear the voices of the people talking inside. It felt dangerous. Someone could spot me or hear me moving. Someone could come out and surprise me while I slept.

Tired as I was, I forced myself to move on.

I was about two miles away from Spring Hill when I saw the church. It was an old one, but I'd never seen it before. It stood on a stretch of open grass, pressed close to a cluster of hickory and pine trees. In the moonlight, its white clapboards showed gray streaks where the paint had worn away. It had red cedar on the pitched roof and gray shingles at the top of the steeple. At first, as I approached, I thought it might be abandoned. But as I got closer, I saw the sermon sign and it was up-to-date. The preacher was going to give a sermon next Sunday called "Be Not Afraid." It sounded like good advice. I wished I could take it.

I tried the front door. Locked. But it was only a padlock, looped through a hasp. The hasp was screwed into the wood of the jamb. The wood looked old and soft. As soon as I pulled at the door, the hasp started to tear away. I pulled harder, making the hasp rattle. The screws started to come out. Every time I yanked at the door, the hasp got looser. Finally, there was a ripping noise and a rattle of screws. The hasp came off and the door swung open.

I went into the church and pulled the door closed behind me.

There was a deep quiet inside, but it was surprisingly bright. The windows were tall and the moon shone through on one side, painting the place silver with deep gray shadows. There wasn't much to see. No decorations or anything. Just pews and a pulpit and an altar with a cross hanging on the wall behind it. And words above the cross: "Put on the full armor of God, so that when the day of evil comes, you may be able to stand your ground."

That sounded like good advice too.

I made my way carefully down the side aisle, moving slowly, reaching out in front of me so I wouldn't bump into anything. I found a door near the pulpit and went through. There was a small changing room. There was a narrow corridor lined with hanging robes. I pushed between the robes until I made out a door standing open at the end. A bathroom.

I turned on the light in there. Found the sink. I ran the faucet and filled my hands with water and brought it to my mouth and gulped it down. I did it again and again.

I never wanted to stop. I felt energy rising inside me as the water filled me.

When I was done, I turned the lights off again. I didn't want anyone passing by to wonder who was inside. I made my way back down the corridor, out of the changing room, back through the door behind the pulpit. I picked a pew for myself, a pew under a window with the moonlight falling directly onto it. I sat on it heavily. Then, exhausted, I lay down on my side, my shoulder against the hard wood.

It was cold—cold and damp too. I turned up my collar. I put my hands under my cheek and pulled my arms in tight against me. After a while, with my chin tucked into my fleece, I felt warmer, warm enough to get some sleep anyway.

But I didn't sleep. Not right away. As exhausted as I was, my mind wouldn't stop working. Images kept flashing at me. The man with the knife in the library bathroom. The thugs who nearly hustled me into their car. The police cruisers racing after me on the lonely street. The gunshot that struck so close to me in the alley that it turned my guts to water with fear.

The flashbacks wouldn't stop coming, and with every one my heart raced faster. After a while, tired as I was, I knew I would not be able to sleep. Still lying on the pew,

I reached inside my fleece and found the papers I'd stuffed into the inner pocket: the news stories I'd printed out in the library. I drew them out into the moonlight.

I held the pages up in front of my face, angling them so the silver moonlight played over them and I could read the words. I shuffled through them until I found the head-line I wanted: "Local Teen Found Stabbed to Death."

That was Alex. Alex Hauser. We'd known each other since kindergarten and for years we did just about every-thing together, even studied karate together for a while. Then, when Alex and I were both sixteen, Alex's dad and mom got divorced and his dad moved away to another town.

It hit Alex hard. He'd hear his mom crying in her room all the time and he didn't know how to help her. They didn't have as much money as they used to either. Alex had to move to a different neighborhood and start going to a different school. He and I couldn't hang out together the way we used to. Alex started going around with a lot of not-so-nice friends and doing stuff he shouldn't have been doing. Drinking, stealing, fighting, stuff like that.

While all this was going on, according to my friend Josh, Alex also started hanging out with Beth Summers. Beth was one of the nicest girls I'd ever met, really sweet-natured and always interested in people and kind to them. I guess it's kind of obvious I liked her a lot myself. She and Alex were both working down on Main Street at Blender-Benders for the summer and they started walking home together. Anyway, according to Josh, as Alex started changing, Beth stopped liking him so much and stopped hanging out with him. Later, when the school year got started, I saw my chance and I asked Beth if she'd go out with me sometime and she said yes.

This is all stuff I can remember. Stuff that happened before this weird yearlong darkness came over my brain.

I also remember what happened the night Alex was murdered. I was in the mall parking lot outside my karate studio after a lesson. I was just tossing my bag into the back of my car—my mom's car, really, but I was driving it. Alex and a couple of his not-so-nice friends came up to me. I guess Alex had heard about me asking Beth out. Even though he wasn't seeing Beth anymore, he was pretty angry. At first, it almost looked like he and his pals were going to start a fight with me. But Alex had second thoughts and he kept things cool.

Instead, he got into the car with me. We took a drive together. It was the first time we'd talked in a long while. Alex was about as upset as I'd ever seen him. He told me how it was at his house since his father left and about his mother crying and all that other stuff.

I didn't know what to say. I mean, my family had its problems like everybody, but this sounded really tough, tougher than anything I'd been through. I just tried to listen to him and be encouraging. I tried to get him to keep strong and not give up on things.

I had a card I used to carry with me in my wallet. An index card Sensei Mike had given to me. He'd written something on it, something a former prime minister of Great Britain, Winston Churchill, had said when his country was in danger during World War II:

"Never give in; never give in—never, never, never, never, in nothing great or small, large or petty; never give in except to convictions of honor and good sense. Never yield to force: never yield to the apparently overwhelming might of the enemy."

I tried to get that idea across to Alex. It was easy for me to say, I know, but that doesn't mean it wasn't true. You have to keep going. I've learned that for a fact now. No matter how bad it gets, you have to keep looking for a way through.

But Alex didn't want to hear that. As hard as I tried to be helpful, our conversation turned into an argument, a big one. I'd stopped the car near the Oak Street park at that point. We were still sitting inside, still talking, and the conversation was getting very intense. Alex started saying all this stuff about how everything people told you was a lie and how you couldn't believe in anything and everything had to be torn down and started again. It was crazy stuff as far as I could see, but he said he had all these new friends who agreed with him and he trusted them.

Finally, he got really angry. He told me I didn't know what I was talking about or what he was going through. He got out of the car and I got out after him. He was really yelling at me—so loudly that a woman who was passing by walking her dogs stopped to look at us.

Then Alex ran away. I tried to stop him, but he ran off into the park. That was it. That was all that happened that I saw.

But there was more in this newspaper—this newspaper story I was holding up in the church moonlight. I had to strain to make out the words, but I could read it. According to this, Alex never made it out of the park alive.

There were a couple of kids in the park—that's what the paper said. Their names were Bobby Hernandez and Steve Hassel. They were just a couple of middle-school kids who had gone into the park to smoke and drink beer where no one could see them. They told the newspaper that they heard Alex and me arguing with each other on the street. A few seconds later, they said, they saw Alex come running into the park. He paused under one of the park streetlamps. That's when they saw his face—that's how they could identify him later. After that, they said, he walked off into the shadows. They could still make out the shape of him, though. He seemed just to be standing there, thinking about something.

According to these kids, Bobby and Steve, another guy came up to Alex after a while. This other guy was in the shadows, too, so they never did see his face, but they could see that he and Alex stood talking together as if they knew each other. After a while, these kids said, Alex and this other guy started arguing. The kids couldn't hear what they were saying because they kept their voices low, but they could make out the tense, angry sound of their words.

Finally, said Bobby and Steve, this guy who was talking to Alex stepped in really close to him. He took hold of Alex's shoulder with one hand and his other hand went to Alex's chest. The next thing the kids knew, Alex had dropped to his knees and the other guy was running away, disappearing into the darkness of the park. Then, as the kids watched, Alex pitched over and fell to the ground.

"At first, we didn't know what was going on," Bobby Hernandez told the newspaper.

"We were, like, scared, man," said Steve. " 'Cause we didn't want anyone to know what we were doing in the park."

"But the dude just kept lying there and he didn't move," added Bobby, "so finally we had to go over and see what was wrong."

What was wrong was that Alex had been stabbed in the chest.

"It was intense," said Bobby. "There was blood all bubbling out of him, and his shirt was, like, soaked with blood, all red and everything."

"He couldn't move no more, but he was still breathing," said Steve. "His eyes were all, like, open. And he just kept saying this name over and over again. He just kept saying, 'Charlie, Charlie . . .' "

The kids called 911 on one of their cell phones, but Alex was dead by the time the ambulance arrived.

I lowered the page and let it rest on my chest. There was a lot in the newspaper story I hadn't known before. The day after Alex died—that was the day my life disappeared.

The next morning—what I thought was the next morning but was really a year later—I woke up captured by the Homelanders. All my memories of that missing year were gone.

How do you know if you're the good guy or the bad guy?

I lay there on the pew. I stared up at the window, up at the half-moon in the sky with the clouds blowing by beneath it. I thought about Alex, about him lying on the ground with the blood coming out of his chest. I thought about him whispering my name with his last breaths. I remembered how we had been kids together and played ball in the streets and played video games and went to the movies. It hurt to think of him, lying there like that, gasping my name out to strangers as he died.

I remembered what I did the rest of that day. At least I thought I did. I remembered how I went home and did my homework and IM'd with Josh and talked to Rick on the phone. I even remembered going to bed. Wouldn't I have remembered if I'd done anything to hurt Alex?

I mean, wouldn't I?

I wasn't sure anymore. Maybe I didn't remember. Maybe something snapped inside me and it was such a shock that I forgot it all. The police said I killed him. The jury said so after listening to all the evidence. Maybe I was a murderer. Maybe I belonged in prison, the way everyone said I did. Maybe when the cops tried to capture me next time, I shouldn't run away at all but just give myself up.

But down deep in my heart, down deep in every part of me, I just couldn't believe it. I knew I was not that guy. No matter how angry I got at Alex, I wouldn't stab him, kill him. That was crazy. I wouldn't kill anyone. I wouldn't hurt anyone, not unless I absolutely had to. That was something I learned in church all the time, something I learned in karate class all the time, something Sensei Mike drilled into my head. Blessed are the peacemakers. Even if someone slaps you, turn the other cheek. Do everything you can to avoid a fight—everything—walk away if you have to, even if people call you a coward, even if you *feel* like a coward. The only time you fight is if there's no other choice. If you have to defend yourself or someone else or if you have to defend something even more important than yourself, like your freedom or someone else's freedom. I believed that was right. I believed it a hundred percent. I couldn't remember the entire year after my argument with Alex, and because I couldn't remember and because the police were after me and the court had found me guilty, I was afraid; I suspected the worst of myself. But whenever I looked into my own heart, I knew I hadn't killed him.

At least, I thought I knew it.

About a month before this, the police had caught me and arrested me. They were about to put me in a car to take me back to prison. But just before I got in, someone—I don't know who—someone in the crowd around me—loosed my handcuffs so I could escape. At the same time, he whispered something in my ear.

He whispered, "You're a better man than you know. Find Waterman."

You're a better man than you know.

I had to believe that. I had to believe I wasn't a killer. I had to believe I could find this Waterman and clear my name. It was all I had to hang on to.

I lay there staring up at the moon. I didn't know where to begin looking for this Waterman. I didn't even know who he was. But I knew where to begin looking for proof of my innocence.

I had to go back—back to Spring Hill. I had to find out what really happened to Alex. I knew the police would be waiting for me there. I knew they would be looking for me. I would have to keep low, keep away from them. And I would have to keep away from my friends too. The last thing I wanted was to get them involved in this, get them into any danger or trouble.

But if there was proof that I wasn't a murderer, that's where it would be: Spring Hill. If there was proof that I was a murderer . . . well, it would be there too. Either way, whatever the truth was, I had to find it.

I closed my eyes. I started to say a prayer. I started to ask God to help me figure out what to do next.

Before I could finish, I was asleep.

PART TWO

CHAPTER TWELVE

Homecoming

I woke up in the dark. After weeks on the run, I'd taught myself to do that. When you're a fugitive, you can't waste the dark. It's precious. In the dark, you can travel. You can go from place to place unseen. If the sun catches you sleeping, you can be discovered. Once the sun rises, you're exposed, you're a target. You have to take advantage of the dark.

I was shivering with cold as I stumbled back to the bathroom. I washed up as best I could and got ready to go. As I stepped out of the church into the chilly darkness, I realized that I knew exactly where I was headed. An idea had come to me while I slept. I guess that was the answer to my prayer.

I knew now where I could go, where I could hide out in Spring Hill from both the police and my friends.

I traveled quickly, skirting the woods, crossing the fields. As I got closer to town, the buildings grew closer together. I passed a small airport, then a school, then a housing development with plenty of empty lots full of overgrown grass. I was still staying off the roads, but I couldn't get very far from them anymore. They were always visible, the headlights rushing by in the dark. The whisper of moving traffic reached me everywhere.

I'd drunk my fill of water in the church bathroom before I left, but the hunger came back to me now and it came back full force. I had to find something to eat in a big hurry or I wasn't going to be able to go on much longer.

I had money—the two hundred dollars I'd taken off the knife-man in the library. But spending it wasn't going to be easy. My run-in with the police in Whitney would've been on the TV news and in the morning papers. There'd be pictures of me all over town. It was too risky for me to try to go into a store. The chances I'd be recognized were just too great.

So I looked for a vending machine. I remembered there were some outside a bowling alley I'd been to a few times. Sure enough, they were still there. I stocked up on peanut-butter crackers and chips and chocolate bars. Not exactly health food, but it was all they had and I was starving. When I thought I had enough, I took it all out into the darkest part of the parking lot and sat cross-legged on the pavement and stuffed as much of it into my face as I could. What was left—not much, a chocolate bar or two—I saved in the pockets of my fleece for later.

I traveled on. As I got closer to the edge of town, everything began to be more familiar. I saw a mall I used to hang out in sometimes. I saw a movie theater I used to go to. There was a gas station I sometimes used.

It was a weird feeling to see these things and remember. I felt as if I were my own ghost haunting the places I used to live. It made me ache inside. When I had lived here, when I'd had my ordinary life, believe me, I didn't wake up every morning and shout hooray or anything like that. I didn't thank heaven every day for how lucky I was. I would've felt like an idiot doing stuff like that. It was just home to me. It was just life. It was just ordinary.

But now, shivering out here in the dark, with the whole world my enemy—now every memory had a sort of golden light around it. I felt as if every minute I'd lived here had been beautiful and blessed. There was so much I couldn't remember—a whole year gone. But there was so much else, so many other years, and they all came flooding back to me.

I passed streets where I used to ride my bike when I was twelve years old. I passed a ball field where I used to watch Alex play Little League so we could grab an ice cream after the game. I saw my elementary school, a long, low gray building that hadn't changed in all the years I'd lived here. I saw a pizza place where Josh and Rick and Miler and I used to meet to plan our strategy for mock trial class.

It was all just ordinary when it happened. But now I ached for those days. It was like a weight inside me, like an anvil or an anchor sitting in my midsection. I felt heavy and slow as I dragged it along with me, moving closer and closer to the center of town.

Soon I was nearing my old neighborhood, moving past familiar houses in the darkness under the trees. I had a tremendous urge to go visit my own house. I don't know why. It wasn't really mine anymore. My parents weren't there. They had moved away after I was sent to prison. Whoever had moved in after them had probably changed everything. Painted it a different color or whatever. It would probably be a pretty depressing sight to see. All the same, I wanted to see it so badly, the pull was almost irresistible.

But I couldn't go. I couldn't risk it. The sky was still dark, but I knew the dawn was coming. You can smell the dawn. You can feel it in the air, hear it in the way the birds start singing. That was another thing I'd learned in my weeks on the run.

So I turned away, headed in a different direction.

I went through more residential neighborhoods. They were empty at this hour, all the houses dark. I moved from front lawn to front lawn, keeping off the sidewalks in case a police car passed by, but keeping out of the backyards, too, because some people keep their dogs back there—another thing I'd learned about being on the run.

I passed into a sort of run-down section of town. The houses were smaller here, and they weren't kept up so well. There were places that hadn't been painted in a while and others with plastic covering the windows. Some of the porches were practically crumbling. Some of the lawns were littered with garbage and old appliances and car parts and so on.

A little farther, I came to some lots with no houses on them at all. Places where there used to be houses but now nothing was left but foundations and rubble, grass and garbage. Beyond these, there was an empty field with an old road leading through a stand of pines. The macadam on the road was practically broken to rubble. It crunched beneath my feet as I walked under the trees.

At the end of the road was the iron gate. Beyond the iron gate was the Ghost Mansion.

CHAPTER THIRTEEN

A Haunting

That's what we called it anyway. Josh and Miler and Rick
and I. We had always called it that. All the kids did. Its
real name was the McKenzie house. It had once belonged
to a rich guy—a guy named McKenzie, I guess. He owned
a factory or something back before I was born.

In those days, this had been the fancy part of town, but
now it was practically deserted. The house was deserted
too. It had been for as long as I could remember. For as
long as I could remember, there had been nothing behind
these iron gates but a looming wreck of a building. It was

three stories tall with some attic rooms in places. There were gloomy gables and black bay windows and a tower with a mansard roof. The whole jumbled structure sat on the top of a little rise of grass, and its black, broken windows seemed like dead eyes staring down at the world. It was as if the place was just watching and waiting for someone to come near it so it could . . . Well, I don't know what, but it wouldn't be good. If ever a house was made to be haunted, this was the house. It even had a little graveyard in back. I guess that's where the McKenzie family laid their dead to rest.

Now, there's a reason I knew this place so well and it had to do with Mr. Sherman again, my history teacher. This was two years ago. He was teaching a class about the Salem Witch Trials. If you don't know about the witch trials, they happened back in colonial days, before America became a country. There were all these hysterical girls running around screaming that witches were after them and they started off a sort of panic of fear through Massachusetts and other parts of New England. A lot of regular people suddenly got accused of being witches. Some of them were put in prison and about twenty or twenty-five of them were killed. Later, when all the panic passed, people realized they'd lost their senses and done a terrible thing, killing their neighbors for no reason.

Now, to me, this was a very interesting story. It was a reminder that you should never let yourself get swept away by the crowd. Sometimes everyone you know can be saying something or believing something and it can just be dead wrong. All around you there might be people getting all excited or panicked and yelling for you to do the wrong thing or believe the wrong thing. They can make it very hard for you to refuse them or even just disagree with them out loud. People get angry at you when you disagree with them—especially when they're wrong—and nobody likes to be unpopular or have people angry at them. Sometimes it takes a lot of courage to use your reason and your heart and stand up for what's true—and I guess not enough people did that during the Salem Witch Trials. That's what I got out of it anyway.

But, of course, for Mr. Sherman the message was different. For him, the Salem Witch Trials proved that religion is bad. See, the people in Salem at the time were Puritans, very strictly religious. So since they were the ones who put the witches on trial, that proved to Mr. Sherman that religion was the whole problem. I think I may already have mentioned that Mr. Sherman was kind of a doofus.

Anyway, Mr. Sherman gave us an assignment. The assignment was to research a superstition and show why it was untrue. Now, on the face of it, I thought this was a pretty cool assignment. It sounded like fun. But we all knew Mr. Sherman. And we all knew if you wanted to get a really top grade, you had to do stuff that he agreed with. In other words, we all knew that if we wanted an A on this assignment, we had to pick some religious belief and show why it was superstitious.

This presented a problem for Rick Donnelly. Rick, as I said, was willing to say just about anything to get good grades so he could go to a really good college. But Rick and I went to the same church and neither of us felt we'd ever heard anything superstitious there. In fact, the stuff we'd learned there had been really helpful in just living ordinary life. So he didn't want to attack his own religion. And it seemed kind of impolite to attack somebody else's. So he didn't really feel right about this assignment at all. It really bothered him.

We talked about it in the cafeteria at lunch at our table with Josh and Miler.

"Look," I said, "there are plenty of superstitions. Black cats. Friday the thirteenth. Write about one of those. That's what I'm going to do."

"You know that's not what he's looking for," said Rick gloomily. He was a tall guy, one of the tallest in the school. His big face was the color of chocolate. It usually looked a lot more cheerful. "I mean, it's all right for you, Charlie. You argue with Sherman all the time, and you don't care when he gives you lower marks."

He was wrong about that. I did care. I cared a lot. But I wasn't going to lie just to get Sherman to give me better grades.

We were all silent for a while. Then I had an idea.

"Hey, you know what would be so cool?" I said. "What if we went and spent a whole night in the McKenzie mansion?"

"What?" said Rick.

"Yeah, yeah," I said, getting more enthusiastic as I thought about it. "We spend the night there and prove there are no ghosts, that it's not haunted. We prove that's just a local superstition."

Josh Lerner cleared his throat. Josh looked like the geek he was: short and kind of slump-shouldered with curly hair and big, thick glasses and a quick, nervous smile. Josh could be kind of a dork at times, but somehow you couldn't help liking him anyway.

"You know, Charlie, that's a very creative thought," he

said. "And it raises an interesting question: Are you out of your ever-loving mind?"

I laughed. "Why shouldn't we? We just take some sleeping bags and camp out for the night and go home and write a report about it. We could take pictures and make recordings and everything and do a whole presentation. The thing is, it would be so cool that Sherman would have to give us an A. He'd have to—or he'd have to explain why."

"He would," murmured Rick, nodding to himself. "I mean, it would just be that cool."

"It would be cool," said Josh, "but you're leaving something out."

"What?"

"The part where we get so terrified we have heart attacks and die."

"I could see where that would cut into the coolness factor," said Miler Miles. Miler was a small, thin guy with short blond hair over a long face. You only had to look at him to know he was going to be some big corporate muck-a-muck when he grew up.

"Why should we be terrified?" I said. "We'd all be together. We'd have flashlights, cell phones . . ."

"Garlic, silver bullets, wooden stakes," Miler added.

"I think I'm having a heart attack already," said Josh. "Really. I'm serious. I can feel it."

As Josh gripped his chest with a worried look in his eyes, Rick nodded. "I'd do it," he said quietly.

"Sure," said Miler with a shrug. "I'd do it too."

"I can't believe I'm hearing this," said Josh. "I can't spend the night in the Ghost Mansion. I have a nervous condition."

I looked at him. "What nervous condition?"

"I'm nervous about spending the night in the Ghost Mansion."

I laughed again. "Well, you don't have to do it then. You're not even in Sherman's class."

"Oh, right. I'm gonna let you guys go and me stay home—like that'd ever happen." Josh gave an elaborate sigh. "All right, all right. I'm in. Just mention how brave I was at my funeral."

So we decided to do it. Josh and Rick and I decided anyway. In the end, Miler said he couldn't do it because he was training for a track meet and needed his sleep. The assignment was due on Monday, so we went out to the mansion on Friday evening.

Now, I have to be honest here and say we didn't exactly get permission from our parents for this. It just wasn't a serious possibility. There were all sorts of signs around the Ghost Mansion saying it was private property and warning you to keep out and that you were entering at your own risk and so on. I was pretty sure that would make my father say no. He'd be all worried about lawsuits or whatever. As for my mother—well, she'd be worried about everything. She was like that. I mean, she worried about me going to school. I might fall out of my desk and land on my pencil or something—I don't know. She just found things to worry about. I knew there was no way she would let me do this.

It's not like I was going to lie about it or anything. I was just going to tell the truth a little late, that's all. I told my parents I was going to have a sleepover with Josh and Rick—I just didn't say where. Later, when we came home, I figured I would sort of just casually mention that little part of it. I didn't expect to get away with it altogether. I thought I might get grounded for a weekend or something. But once my parents knew we were all right and understood why we'd done it in the first place, I thought I would get off pretty easily.

Anyway, off to the mansion we went just before sunset. We had our sleeping bags and flashlights, our cell phones—which we could also use as cameras—and a little

MP3 recorder I had. Josh even brought his Sony PSP so we'd have something to do if we got bored.

It was easy to get inside the house. The heavy front door was locked, but there were plenty of other doors that were open. We found a big empty room—a parlor— on the second floor and set ourselves up in there. Then we took a look around so we could take some pictures.

The place was pretty spooky, I have to say. The rooms were mostly empty, but now and then you'd find an ancient sofa or a dresser or something—just standing there alone in a room as if it was waiting for someone to come in and use it. The windows were all broken so the wind came through, making the dust shift on the floors and the spiderwebs wave back and forth in the corners. There were these creepy noises, too, every once in a while: little footsteps. Mice in the walls. That's what we told ourselves anyway.

But it wasn't until the night came down that the real, serious creepiness set in. The house sort of settled around us then, making all sorts of little creaks and pops that sounded like somebody walking around. The mice went crazy, running here and there in the walls. Some even came out and we would jump when we saw them suddenly scampering past the doorway. The wind picked up.

It played in the branches outside, making the trees whisper and groan as it went past.

But the spookiest thing of all was the graveyard.

In the upstairs parlor where we were, there were two big windows on one wall, the panes half-broken. When we went to stand in front of one of them and peered out through the jagged shards of glass, we had a full view of the McKenzie family cemetery in the back. It was a scary sight to see.

The night was clear, but there was only a sliver of a moon. At first, when we looked out, all we could see were the trees, their great spread of naked branches black against the starlit sky. The grass below them was in deeper darkness. But after only a moment or so, our eyes adjusted and the shapes of the graves came clear.

They were mostly headstones, about a dozen of them. But there were also a few obelisks here and there. Then, off to the right, there was a statue, just one statue, all alone. It was a statue of a woman with a sort of hood over her head, a cowl. You couldn't make out her face in the dark at this distance. But she was making a gesture with her hand, reaching out as if trying to stop someone from leaving.

"Look at that," said Rick quietly. "Weird, huh?"

I used my flashlight to try to pick out the statue's face. The light just barely reached her, but its faint ray brought her figure out of the darkness so that it seemed more real somehow, almost alive.

"Stop doing that," said Josh.

I turned the flashlight off quickly.

"She looks like someone she loved just died," I said. "She looks like she's sort of reaching out because she wants to stop him from leaving her and moving off into the land of death."

"Okay," said Josh. "Now that's the single most frightening thing anyone has ever said."

"Maybe we should stop standing here looking at her," Rick suggested.

"Yeah," I said.

"Yeah," said Josh.

We moved away from the window, back into the room.

We took a few more pictures to prove we'd been here and everything. Then I made some recordings, talking about what it was like to be in the house and how spooky it was. Then we passed the PSP around for a while until the batteries started to run low. Finally, the best idea seemed to be to get into our sleeping bags.

Lying in the bags, we went on talking for a while, but only for a while. We were all getting tired and the thing was, none of us wanted to be the last person left awake. That would've been too much like being alone. None of us wanted to be alone in this place.

Luckily, I was tired and I fell asleep pretty quickly.

Unluckily, it didn't last.

After about an hour, I suddenly found myself wide awake without knowing why. Had I heard a noise? I propped myself up on my elbow and listened. Nothing—well nothing, that is, except for the whispering wind in the trees and the creaking of the house and those quick little footsteps in the walls.

I used my flashlight to check my watch. It was about one fifteen in the morning. I quickly passed the flashlight beam over Rick and Josh. They were fast asleep, totally unconscious, their mouths wide open with soft snores coming out of them.

My heart sank. I felt totally alone.

All right, I told myself, *don't get stupid. There are no ghosts here. That's just a superstition. That's the whole point of the project, right?*

Right. I lay down again, pulled my sleeping bag up around me. I listened to the house creaking and the mice running and the trees whispering and a low groan that was almost lost in the wind ...

I sat up quickly, my heart hammering hard.

A low groan? What in the world was that?

For a long moment I sat completely still, tense, listening as hard as I'd ever listened in my life. There was nothing. The creaking, the mice, the wind ... There wasn't any groan. There couldn't have been any groan. I began to convince myself that it was just my imagination.

Then I heard it again. A deep, complaining moan. It was coming through the window. It was coming from outside. It was coming from the direction of the cemetery.

I stopped breathing. Long seconds passed. I told myself I was imagining things. I told myself to lie back down, to close my eyes, go to sleep, forget about it.

But there was no way. No way.

I worked myself out of the sleeping bag and stood up, my flashlight gripped tightly in my sweaty hand. I'd taken my sneakers off before getting in the bag. I slipped my feet back into them now, though I didn't go to the trouble of tying them. Picking my way with the flashlight, I moved carefully to the window.

The moon had gone down. I could just barely make out the shadowy fingers of the tree branches against the starlight, but below, in the cemetery, the darkness was almost complete. My eyes strained as I tried to pick out the stones and obelisks and the statue. I could trace their shapes only faintly in the deep shadow.

There were no more groans. Only the wind. The stirring of branches. The rattle of leaves.

I was about to turn away. But before I did, I raised the flashlight and shone its beam out into the night.

The dim ray picked out a headstone not far from the house. I shifted the flashlight to the side and another headstone became visible, then another. Finally, the light rested on the black base of the statue. I raised it slowly and the mourning woman in her cowl came into view.

I gazed down at her where she stood ghostly and pathetic and still.

And slowly, I became aware that there was another figure standing just behind her.

It was a vague outline beyond the reach of the light. The figure of a man standing motionless, his face upraised and turned toward me. It was a weird, empty face. It seemed to have no features. It seemed to gleam bizarrely in the darkness.

My heart sped up. I started to move the light to get a better view.

Suddenly, a hand grabbed my shoulder. I cried out and dropped the flashlight. Its beam rolled crazily this way and that around the room.

"What're you doing?"

It was Rick, standing behind me.

"Oh! Oh!" was all I could say. My heart was pounding so hard I thought it would explode.

"What?" muttered Josh from his sleeping bag—and both Rick and I jumped, startled by the sound of his voice.

"There's someone . . ." I managed to whisper finally. "Someone out there."

"Out where?" Rick whispered back.

"In the graveyard."

Rick had his flashlight too. He shone it out the window. "I don't see anyone."

"By the statue. Just behind it."

"There's no one there."

I looked. He was right. The figure was gone.

Josh had his sneakers on too now. He joined us at the window.

"What was he doing?" said Rick.

"Just standing there. Just staring up at me," I said.

"Who?" said Josh.

"I don't know. Someone out in the night. In the cemetery."

"There was someone in the cemetery staring up at you?"

"Yeah."

"That's terrifying," said Josh. "I mean, that's . . . that's terrifying. I mean, it's terrifying. Isn't it?"

I nodded.

"I mean, isn't that terrifying?" said Josh.

"All right, man," said Rick. "I think we all get that it's terrifying."

"I wanted to make sure it wasn't just me."

"It's not just you." Rick moved his flashlight over the graveyard. The wind rose, the trees bending and creaking. We stood together, staring, as Rick's beam picked out a headstone, an obelisk, and then the mourning woman making her eerie gesture to the darkness. But there was nothing else in the graveyard now. No figure lurking in the deeper shadows. "Is it possible you could've . . . ?"

"Imagined it?" I said. "I don't think so, bro. I heard it first. I heard this . . . this kind of groan."

"A groan?" said Josh, his voice breaking. "What do you mean, a groan?"

"I mean, like a . . . like a low groan, like, 'O-o-o-oh.' Like that."

"That is so terrifying," Josh murmured.

"Then I got up and came to the window. And when I looked out . . . I only saw it for a split second, but it was definitely there. A figure. A man, I think. With this kind of weird, white face . . ."

"A weird, white face? A weird, white face? What does that even mean?"

"It means a weird, white face, Josh. Like it . . . I don't know. Like it didn't have any features."

"How could it not have features? What kind of face is that? If it's a face it has to have features. Otherwise, it would be terrifying. Right? I mean, isn't that . . ."

The words caught in his throat as the wind became even stronger and the whisper and creak of the branches grew louder and under that whisper—yes, there it was again: that low, dreadful groan as of a man in pain.

Rick and Josh and I fell silent, gaping at one another with open mouths.

"Did you . . . ?" Josh tried to say.

Rick and I nodded. We'd heard it too.

We turned toward the window, all three of us. All three of us shone our flashlights through the broken glass and out over the deep darkness. The darkness shifted and whispered with the night wind.

Before I knew I was thinking it, I heard myself say, "We have to take a look. We have to go out there."

"Right," said Josh. "Because we're not frightened enough. Because there's still a slim chance my hair won't turn white and I won't spend the rest of my life locked in a padded room cackling uncontrollably. Go out there? What are you talking about? Are you crazy?"

"I saw something," I said. "Someone—something—I don't know. We have to go and find out what it was."

"Why? We could stay here instead. We could not find out. It could be, like, an unsolved mystery."

But Rick understood. "That's the project," he said. "We came here to prove this place isn't haunted, that that's just a local superstition. If we don't investigate, we won't really know."

"I can live with that," said Josh. "Really. I'm strangely content just as I am."

"Yeah, but we're the ones who have to give the report," I said. "The whole point was to force Sherman to give us an A by doing something too cool for him to ignore. If we don't follow through, it won't happen. You can stay here," I told Josh. "But we've got to take a look."

I knelt down to tie my sneakers. Rick did the same.

"Oh, I can stay here," said Josh. "In the haunted house. Alone. By myself. Thanks. You're too generous. No, really." He knelt and tied his sneakers, too, muttering to himself the whole time.

It's funny—I mean, funny as in strange—in these last few weeks, I'd faced so many dangers, and I'd been afraid, more afraid than I like to think about or say. But I don't think I've been as fearful, before or since, as I was that night Rick, Josh, and I went out into the graveyard behind the McKenzie mansion.

We crept downstairs, our shoulders bumping together as we followed our flashlight beams down a long hall toward the back of the house. We came into a bare room lined with old, broken cabinets and shelves. It must have been the kitchen once. As we stepped in, we heard pattering footsteps. Small, furry bodies dashed out of sight as the light came near them.

Our beams picked out a door. We moved toward it.

When we stepped out of the house, we stopped and stood stock-still, all three of us. Inside, our flashlights together had seemed almost bright, lighting our way easily. Here, though, the night felt vast around us. It seemed to swallow the beams and drown them in nothingness.

We stayed where we were. We stared. We were afraid to move away from the house, afraid if we got too far from it, we would not be able to escape back inside.

The trees moved and murmured above us. The sky seemed dizzyingly far away. The dark seemed dizzyingly deep.

"All right," I said. But I didn't step forward.

"All right," said Rick. But he didn't move either.

"This is terrifying," said Josh.

We stiffened, listening. There was a fresh rattle of dead leaves as the wind blew them tumbling over the earth in front of us. The sound made us lift our flashlight beams over the sparse grass and shine them in the direction of the noise.

One beam—Rick's, I think—touched on a white stone—a headstone—the headstone nearest to the house. There was the graveyard, barely twenty yards ahead of us.

It seemed until then that I'd forgotten how to breathe. I remembered now and drew in a deep breath.

"All right," I said again.

I started moving forward. Josh was to my left, Rick was to my right. They started moving, too, just behind me.

As we advanced, our flashlight beams trembled over the small field of stones. I was aware of an awful sense of suspense as I waited for the terrible moment when one of the beams would pick out the figure with the gleaming, featureless face.

Then, suddenly, Josh's beam fell on the statue of the mourning woman. Even though I knew it was just a statue, the sight of her up close like that was still a shock. She seemed to float out of the darkness at us like a ghost. I could make out her face now, the staring, empty eyes, the parted, fearful lips that seemed about to whisper, "No. Don't go." And her hand, that gesturing hand . . . You could almost sense the presence of the dead spirit she was trying to hold on to. You could almost see it moving away in the black air before her.

Josh saw the statue and stopped in his tracks, gaping up at it. I heard him swallow hard. He kept his flashlight trained on the woman's face, as if he couldn't force his hand to move.

I took one look at her, then looked away. Still, I could feel her staring down at me with those cold, marble eyes as I kept walking toward her, kept walking toward the place where I'd seen that other figure, the weird, faceless presence.

The mourning woman loomed over me as I got closer and closer to her. Then, a few feet away from her, I stopped. It was too much. Her presence was too eerie. The dark beyond her was just too deep. The possibility of coming upon that featureless man I'd seen staring up at me was just too real. I was afraid to go any farther.

I was about to announce that there was nothing there. About to turn back.

But then I spotted something—something lying on the ground. My passing flashlight picked out a little patch of white. I moved the beam around until I found it again.

"Look," I said.

My friends closed ranks around me. Their flashlight beams joined mine. We stared down. There was a dry branch lying in the leaves just on the far side of the statue, just a few feet away from the statue's base. The stick had snapped in half and the white core of it stood out against the brown background of the dirt and leaves.

"See that stick?" I said. "It's broken. Like someone stepped on it." I moved my beam around the stick. I couldn't be sure, but it seemed to me there were other disturbances, discolorations in the leaves where they had been overturned, their damp undersides facing upward.

"Broken stick," said Rick softly. "Doesn't have to mean anything . . ."

"I know," I said. "But look at the leaves too. It looks like someone was walking there."

I'll never be sure where I found the courage, but all at once I was walking forward again, moving away from Rick and Josh. The mourning woman was right above me now, staring down at me as I moved alongside her—and then past her. I went to the broken stick. I bent down and picked it up. I straightened, holding the stick in one hand and the flashlight in the other. Turning the stick this way and that, examining it under the light.

And as I did, I felt a hand snake up from the earth and wrap its cold fingers around my ankle.

I'm embarrassed now when I remember the shriek I let out. And I shrieked again as I tore my ankle free and stared down to see a white, featureless face gleaming up at me from the ground.

In a single, swift movement, the uncanny figure leapt to its feet in front of me, its hands lifted in the air, its fingers curled like claws.

And it shouted, "Boo!"

Because it was Miler, of course. Who else could it have been?

CHAPTER FOURTEEN
The Return

Josh, Rick, and I did not beat Miler to death and bury his mangled body in a shallow grave with a headstone warning future would-be practical jokers that this could be their fate. We wanted to, believe me. And he deserved it, that's for sure. I can't even remember now why we decided to let him live. He'd brought some brownies his mother had made—maybe that was it. Or maybe it was because he also brought an extra PSP with a battery pack that would last till dawn and keep us from having to go to sleep again. That was important, too, because at the time, there didn't seem to be any chance we'd be able to sleep again—ever—so a little gaming seemed like it might be a good way to pass the time.

Anyway, for whatever reason, we let Miler live and he took off the plastic mask he'd used to hide his features and joined us in the house and told us all about how he didn't really have a track meet to train for but had just come up with this awesome idea for a practical joke that was sure to scare the daylights out of us. Which, after the terror had passed, we were forced to admit had worked pretty well and had, in retrospect, been incredibly terrifying while being kind of hilarious at the same time. And yes, I was also forced to admit that I had screamed like a girl when Miler grabbed my ankle and that that had also been more or less hilarious. In fact, as I recall, I was forced to admit this several times before I finally punched Josh in the arm to get him to shut up about it.

Mostly, we spent the rest of the night laughing until we couldn't breathe and then breathing enough so we could start laughing again. On top of which, the story of Miler's prank made for such a good report that Mr. Sherman was, in fact, forced to give us the As we were looking for. And that, in turn, got my parental sentence reduced from two weeks grounded to one Saturday cleaning out the garage.

That hadn't been that long ago. A year and a half or so—not that long in the scheme of things. But it seemed to me like another life.

Now, I had come back to the old McKenzie place. I didn't have much choice. I had to try to clear my name. I couldn't let the police find me, and I couldn't let my friends get involved and put themselves in danger. The Ghost Mansion was the only place I could think of where I could hide long enough to get the job done. No one ever came here. No one even passed by. No one would have any reason to suspect that they would find me here.

The iron gate that blocked the way in was held shut by a chain, but the chain was wrapped only loosely through the bars. When I pushed against the gate, the chain slid off and dangled between the bars. I opened the gate wide enough for me to squeeze through.

I started up the last stretch of the path to the Ghost Mansion.

It was dark and cold as dawn approached. The half-moon that had shone through the church window earlier that night was low to the horizon now, sinking out of sight behind the faraway trees. The last dark of night seemed to gather around me. I had a small keychain flashlight in my pocket. I took it out and pressed its button occasionally to send a thin white beam down at the path. It wasn't much light, but it was enough to keep me headed in the right direction.

By now, the broken macadam of the road was all but gone. There was nothing left but dirt and stones. They crunched under my sneakers as the path dipped down into a small valley and then rose again.

I climbed up over the crest of the little hill and finally saw the house.

It hadn't changed any. It still loomed large and tumbledown and gloomy on the top of the rise. It still stared out at the darkness through its broken windows as if waiting for victims to approach. The predawn wind still moved over the surrounding fields, still stirred the trees and the unmown grass so that the place almost seemed a living presence, restless and murmuring. It was all just as I remembered it.

But if the house hadn't changed, I had. I'd changed a lot. The last time I'd come here, I was pretty much just a kid, getting into a little harmless mischief. I was afraid of ghosts then. The noise of mice in the walls made me jump and shiver. A staring statue in a graveyard sent a chill up my spine.

I was older now—a young man, I'd guess you'd call me. Even though I'd lost a year of growing up—even though I couldn't remember it—I had grown up all the same. I was still afraid—I was afraid all the time—but the things that frightened me were different. They were real. Not ghosts, but people—bad people—who didn't believe we should have the freedom to think and say whatever we wanted and live the way we thought was right. They hated America because we had those freedoms. They wanted to hurt our country and they wanted to hurt me. I was afraid of them—the bad guys—and I was afraid of the good guys, the police. The police who wanted to put me in prison for the next twenty-five years. I was afraid they would catch me before I could find out the truth.

So as I walked up the hill toward the Ghost Mansion, my feelings were weird—mixed, I guess would be the best way to describe them. I looked up at that great hulk of a house sitting against the deep blue sky and among the silhouetted trees—I looked up at it and I felt it looking back down at me—and yeah, I have to admit I still felt that old chill, that same chill I'd felt the last time I was here, as if something supernatural, something bizarre and frightening, might be waiting for me behind those black, staring windows.

I felt that—but mostly, I felt something else. I felt sad. I missed those old days, those days I'd last been here. I missed being a kid. I missed being afraid of dumb things that couldn't really hurt me. I missed laughing until I couldn't breathe and then breathing and laughing some more.

I guess the point is that more than anything, I missed my friends. I missed Rick and Miler and Josh. I missed having someone to kid around with and talk to. I missed long conversations about girls and sports and arguments about whether *Medal of Honor* was cooler than *Prince of Persia* and why part 2 of any trilogy was never as good as parts 1 and 3. I missed being with the guys who knew me best and liked me just the way I was. I missed my friends.

But they were gone. I had to face that. Those days were gone and I was alone, as alone and empty as the McKenzie house.

The dark house rose over me as I approached. The autumn branches of the trees leaned down toward me, creaking and groaning as I stepped into the shadow of the doorway.

The last time I'd been here, I remembered, the front door had been locked and we had had to go around to the side before we found a door that was open. Now I just touched the front door and it opened easily, the rotten wood around the latch cracking and giving way.

I stepped inside. The door swung closed behind me with a soft, high moan. I stood in the foyer at the foot of the front stairs as the brooding darkness of the house closed around me.

I was about to reach for my flashlight, but then I noticed: in the time it had taken me to walk up the path, the first faint light of dawn had crept into the sky. That light was filtering to me here from the windows in the living room off to my right. After only a moment or two, my eyes adjusted and I could make out the shapes of things pretty clearly.

I went to the foot of the stairs and peered up into the deep shadows. I put my hand on the banister—and then quickly pulled it away as I felt the slimy dust under my palm. I was about to start upstairs when I hesitated. Did I hear something up there? Was something moving around?

I stood still and listened. The wind was rising the way it does at dawn and it blew freely through the house. The house creaked and settled, just the way it had the last time. And the mice—they were still here as well. In fact, they sounded particularly active. I could hear them scurrying this way and that. I guess they were trying to get back to their nests before daylight.

I smiled to myself, remembering how Josh and Rick and I had lain in our sleeping bags, listening to those same noises, scared out of our wits. Every time we heard a new noise, we would glance at one another nervously and try to explain it away, try to laugh it off and reassure one another. It seemed kind of silly now.

So I started up the stairs again—and stopped again. I had heard something. Something was moving around on the second floor. It wasn't the wind or the house or the mice either. It was bigger than that. I could tell by the way it made the floorboards shift.

I was tense now. My mind was racing, trying to come up with some explanation, trying to make sense of it. I thought it might be the cops or even the Homelanders, waiting for me. But how would they ever think to come here? Maybe it was just some animal, I told myself. Some raccoon who'd gotten stranded. Or maybe it was some homeless guy who'd crept in to get out of the cold and get some sleep.

I thought about turning away. I thought about running. But the sky was getting even brighter and there was really nowhere else to go, nowhere else I could think of anyway.

I waited there a long time, but there was no other noise. I shook my head at myself. Maybe I hadn't grown up as much as I'd thought. I was still afraid of spooks and shadows and strange bumps in the night.

I shrugged it off. It was probably nothing. I started up the stairs again, faster this time, moving with more boldness than I felt.

The dawn was coming quickly now. As I reached the second-floor landing, I could see the new light coming through open doors and spilling into the hallway. I saw windows through the doors, and through the windows I saw the sky growing paler and paler blue. Soon I could make out the walls and the floorboards of the second-story corridor that led to the upstairs parlor, that same large room where I had come to stay the night with my friends all that time ago.

I moved down the corridor to the parlor doorway. The door itself was gone and I saw the window on the wall beyond. The light of the sky was growing brighter even as I watched. Birds were singing and the branches of the trees were coming clear against the brightening blue.

I was about one step away from the threshold when I heard a soft, quick, urgent whisper:

"Coming!"

There was no mistaking it: a human voice. I froze, motionless, my pulse pounding. The thoughts in my head seemed to all come together, like people shouting at each other in an argument: *The police! The Homelanders! They're here! They found me!* I knew I had to run, but for a second I was so startled I couldn't get my body moving.

And before I could budge from the spot, a figure stepped into the doorway in front of me.

The light from the window behind him blotted out his features. He was just a gray form standing there, as motionless as I was.

For a long moment we confronted each other, just like that, neither of us moving a muscle.

Then, slowly, the figure lifted his hands above his head, his fingers curled like claws.

And he said softly, "Boo!"

It was Miler. I couldn't believe it. It was impossible, but it was true: it was Miler Miles.

And now Josh and Rick were there, stepping into the doorway behind him.

And after another moment, Rick said, "Dude. What took you so long?"

CHAPTER FIFTEEN

What Friends Are For

I don't know how long I stood there, staring like an idiot. I'm pretty sure it was a good long time.

Finally, Miler said, "You know, you look really stupid with your mouth hanging open like that. No offense or anything."

Then the next thing I knew I was in the room and we were all together, hugging and slapping hands and slugging one another's shoulders and just saying, "Man!" and "Dude!" and "Bro!" over and over again. I don't think I have ever been so happy to see anybody in my life. I don't even know how to describe the feeling. It was like the dawn came up at the windows and the dawn came up inside me at the same time. It was like I didn't realize how dark it was in my heart until the light shone through.

The light. My friends. I could hardly believe they were here in front of me.

I looked around in a daze. There were sleeping bags on the floor and flashlights and empty soda cans and an empty bag of potato chips. I guess they'd been waiting for me a long time.

"How . . . ?" I finally managed to get the words out. "How did you guys know? How did you know I would come here?"

"Josh knew," said Rick. "He figured it out."

Josh touched his own shoulder with a finger and made a sizzling noise to show just how hot he was.

I answered with a gesture of my own: raising my shoulders and lifting my hands in an enormous shrug as if to say, *What's the story?*

"I saw you on TV," Josh said. "The whole thing about how you were in the library and the librarian called the cops and the cops showed up and started chasing you and everything."

"Yeah?"

"And I thought, well, the last time anyone heard anything about you, you were escaping from the cops all the way over in Centerville. So I knew you were heading this way. I figured you must be coming back to Spring Hill."

"Sure, but . . ." I gestured around me at the big empty parlor. The room—the whole feeling of the house—was growing less and less dismal as the sun poured in through the windows. "The Ghost Mansion. How did you figure I'd come back to the Ghost Mansion?"

Josh gave an almost modest tilt of his head. "I just tried to think the way you'd think. I figured if I knew you were coming to Spring Hill, the cops would know too. That meant it would be dangerous—more dangerous here than anyplace else."

I nodded. He was right. Spring Hill was probably the most dangerous place I could be right now, the place where I was most likely to get caught.

Josh went on: "And if you were coming to the most dangerous place you could be, then you'd have to have a really good reason for it. There'd have to be something really urgent you had to do, something you had to do whether it was dangerous or not. So I thought, *Well, what could that be?* What could you do here you couldn't do anyplace else? And then it came to me: you were coming back here to try to prove your innocence, to try to show it wasn't you who killed Alex."

"That's right," I said. "That's exactly right. I am."

Josh stood a little straighter, proud of himself. "So then I thought, well, if you were gonna prove your innocence, it might take some time, so you'd need a place to stay. Your parents moved to Stanton, so you couldn't stay with them. And I knew you wouldn't come to us because you wouldn't want to get us involved; you wouldn't want us to get in any trouble."

I nodded slowly. "That's right too."

"So where else was there for you to go?" said Josh finally. "What other place did you know around here that was empty and secluded, where you could get shelter during the day, and get into town pretty quickly at night?"

I nodded, impressed. Geeky as he was, Josh had always been the smartest guy in our group.

But as I listened to him, a little of my happiness at our reunion started to fade. I moved to the window. As I passed Josh, I punched him lightly on the arm.

"Good going, Josh," I said softly. "That was really good thinking."

"I guess I'm not as dumb as I look," said Josh with a goofy laugh.

"No one could be as dumb as you look," said Miler.

I stood at the window and looked out. The day had now dawned fully. The bright, pale sky gleamed down through the naked branches of the autumn oaks. The branches swayed in the morning breeze. On the ground below, dead leaves blew through the old McKenzie graveyard. They covered the bases of the stones and the obelisks. They danced around the base of the statue.

She was still there. The cowled, mourning woman. Still staring blankly with her stone eyes, still reaching out in grief as if to stop the soul she loved from departing. She was just as eerie as I remembered her too. Creepy and weirdly alive. It still made me shiver a little to look at her.

I stared down into the graveyard, thinking, troubled.

"What's the matter, bro?" said Rick behind me.

I turned to them. The three of them stood together, looking at me.

They had changed, I could see. A year does a lot to you when you're seventeen. They had changed a lot, just as I had.

Miler was still a small guy, still had the short blond hair and the long face with its sharp, piercing green eyes. But the face seemed darker and more serious now that there was stubble on it. And his runner's body had filled out, become sturdy and muscular. He was wearing jeans and a corded sweater with the sleeves rolled up, and I could see his shoulders had gotten broader and the muscles of his arms had become big and ropy.

And Rick—he still had that big, round, cheerful face—but there was something new in his large eyes, some kind of—I don't know—gentleness and understanding that hadn't been there before. It made him look a lot older. Plus, hard as it was to believe, he was even taller than he had been, and more substantial too. In his jeans and basketball jacket, he looked practically massive.

As for Josh—well, he was a geek forever. He still blinked out from behind his big glasses, still had the pale face and short curly hair and the geeky laugh. But instead of being small and slump-shouldered, he was tall and skinny. And instead of a constant nervous smile, his smile was sort of crooked now and cool—ironic, I guess you'd call it. He looked like he was constantly making fun of himself—and of just about everything else too.

They stood in the middle of the room together, watching me, waiting for me to answer them. I tried to find the right words.

"Well, the thing is— I mean, don't take this the wrong way. It's great to see you guys. I can't tell you how great it is."

"But?" said Miler.

"But Josh is right. I came to the Ghost Mansion because I didn't want to get you involved."

Rick gave a big laugh. He stepped up to me, towering over me, looking down at me from his height. "Hey, Charlie, we understand that. We know you want to keep us out of it. We're just ignoring you, that's all."

"Sure," said Miler. "I mean, that's what friends are for, guy. To figure out what you want and then do exactly the opposite."

I laughed. "That's great of you, really, but . . . this is serious. I mean, this isn't, like, a prank or something, like spending the night here without telling our parents. It's the police that are after me. The real police. I'm a fugitive. They think I'm a killer. If they find out you guys are helping me, you could be accessories or something. You could go to jail."

Rick nodded. He looked over at Miler. "He's right. Let's get out of here."

Miler gave a quick laugh. None of them moved. They weren't going anywhere.

"The thing is, Charlie," Josh said, "we can't leave. You need us. The police are gonna be looking for you everywhere. Everyone in town is gonna be looking for you. You're gonna need help, you're gonna need people who can go out and look around and ask questions without making people suspicious. How else are you gonna find out what really happened to Alex? How else are you gonna prove you're innocent?"

"That's crazy," I said. "It's too dangerous. Besides, you don't even know I really am innocent."

Rick and Miler looked at each other again.

"He's right," Miler said. "Let's get out of here."

Rick laughed. Then he turned to me. "We know you're innocent, Charlie."

Miler nodded. So did Josh.

"We all know it," Rick said.

"Face it," said Miler. "You're just not killer material, old pal."

"Don't get us wrong," Josh added. "You have a lot of other good qualities. I mean, we still like you and everything, even if you're not a murderer. But you're not a murderer."

I turned away and looked out the window again. I had to. I didn't want them to see my face just then, the

138

emotion in my face. The police said I was guilty. The judge and jury said so. The newspapers, the TV. Even I sometimes wondered whether I was really innocent or not.

But not Rick and Miler and Josh. They knew I was innocent. They didn't have a doubt.

When I got my voice back, I said, "It's not that easy. There's more to it than that."

"Like what?" said Rick.

"The police aren't the only ones who are after me. In fact, they're not even the worst of it." I looked from one of them to another, from one waiting gaze to another. "There's some kind of underground group. They call themselves the Homelanders. They tried to assassinate the secretary of Homeland Security."

"Oh yeah," said Rick. "Last month, on the bridge. I heard about that. They said you might have been guilty of that too."

"I wasn't guilty . . ."

"Yeah, yeah, yeah, we know that. But what's it all about?"

"I'm not sure exactly. I know they're terrorists. Foreign. Islamist. Only they recruit homegrown anti-Americans. They think I was one of them . . . What?"

Rick had laughed. "Sorry," he said. "The idea of you

joining a group of anti-Americans. Weren't you, like, born on the Fourth of July or something?"

I had to press my lips together to keep my emotions down. Again, even I had doubts about what had happened to me. Even I wondered: Was I a good guy or a bad guy? But my friends didn't. They didn't wonder at all.

"Well . . . anyway . . ." I finally managed to say. "They think I was one of them and that I betrayed them. They want me dead. And they're dangerous, man. I mean, like, really dangerous. If they figure out that you know where I am, they'll come after you for sure."

"He's right," said Rick to Miler. "Let's get out of here."

"Would you stop?" I said—although I couldn't help laughing myself this time. "This is serious. They're serious. One of them tried to knife me in the library."

"In the library?" said Josh. "Gee, I hope he was quiet about it."

Frustrated, I closed my eyes, lowered my head, pinched the bridge of my nose between my thumb and forefinger. These guys didn't get it. They thought it was all some sort of big joke, some sort of big adventure.

Rick put his hand on my shoulder. "Hey," he said, as if he was reading my mind. "We do get it. We understand. It's real. It's dangerous. And believe me, Charlie, we'd all rather be somewhere else. But what are we gonna do: Leave you out here alone to fend for yourself? Let you get arrested the first time you stick your ugly face out the door? The way I look at it—the way we all look at it—we don't really have any choice. You're our friend, you're in trouble, and you're innocent. So here we are."

I had to turn away again. I looked out the window, down at the cemetery. It was all blurry for a couple of seconds, but when my eyes cleared, I saw the mourning woman again with her blank stare from under her cowl and her grief-stricken gesture at the empty air. So much was gone, I thought to myself. My family, my school days, my safety, my childhood, a year of my life. I'd lost so much.

But not everything. My friends were here. My friends were still here.

"Okay," I said. I turned back to them quickly, speaking brusquely to hide my emotions. "Okay, if that's the way you want it . . . But if we're gonna do this, we gotta do it right."

"Okay," said Rick. The others nodded. "Like how?"

"Well," I said. "Like, how did you all get here?"

"We parked over in the Lake Center Mall," said Miler. "Then we cut through the housing development to those

141

woods back there. No one could've followed us without our seeing them."

"Good," I said. I took a few pacing steps into the room. "That's really good. You gotta do stuff like that every time you come. Change things up. Make sure no one's watching."

"Okay," said Rick. "What else?"

"Well, you can't tell anyone. Not anyone." I looked at them, searched their faces. "The more people who know, the more danger there is. No matter who it is, no matter how much you may think you can trust them, you can't tell them I'm here or that you're working with me. Not your parents, not your teachers, not your girlfriends, no one."

There was a long silence in answer. Miler and Rick looked at each other and Josh looked at both of them and then they looked at me.

I felt something sink inside me. They'd already told someone.

"What?" I said.

They all looked away.

"Who did you tell? Don't you understand? There's no one else we can trust."

Rick took a deep breath. He screwed one eye shut

and sort of looked off with the other eye at nothing in particular. "There's just one other person," he said.

And just then, as if on cue, I heard the front door open on the first floor. I tensed. I glanced at my friends. They continued to look away from me.

The front door gave the same soft, high moan as before and then a soft thud as it swung shut again. There were footsteps rising quickly up the stairs.

It came to me then. I knew who it was. My breath caught. Suspense pulsed through my body. I turned slowly to face the door.

The footsteps crested the stairs and came down the hall toward us. I saw her in the shadows first, her figure obscure but still recognizable. And then my breath came back and something—my heart, I guess—seemed to crack open inside me and a kind of wild heat flooded through my body.

Beth Summers stepped into the doorway and into the light of day that was pouring through the window.

CHAPTER SIXTEEN

Beth

I guess there must be more beautiful girls in the world than Beth, but not to me. I mean, a lot of guys looked at her and kind of shrugged. They thought she was just okay. But not me. I mean, I knew she wasn't gorgeous or glamorous or anything the way some of the other girls in school were. She was of average height with a graceful figure. She had ordinary, honey-brown hair that fell around her face in ringlets. She had small, smooth features: blue eyes, a quick kiss of a mouth.

But somehow, after you talked to her for a while, after

you got to know her, she started to look really awesome. I thought so anyway. After you found out how warm she was, how kind, how interested she was in what other people had to say. It changed the way she looked . . . I don't really know how to describe it.

She was wearing khaki slacks now and a pink sweater and a long blue coat against the autumn chill. She had one of those extra-large purses over her shoulder—I don't know what they call them—a carryall maybe.

She stood there—just stood there—a long time, and I just stood there and we looked at each other, not knowing what to say. It was a strange situation, that's for sure. It was awkward. Really awkward.

On my side, I felt the same way I'd always felt about her. I liked her a lot, more than I knew how to put into words. Back in school, whenever I saw her, I felt a kind of emptiness inside me, as if there were a Beth-shaped hole in me that I hadn't known about until I met her.

But now—now there was a history between us.

See, somehow, during this year, this missing year, Beth and I had fallen in love with each other—but I couldn't remember any of it. I'd won the love of the single sweetest girl I'd ever met, and I couldn't remember how or what it felt like. I couldn't remember our first date or our first kiss. If there were private jokes we had, or secrets we'd shared, they were all gone. We had been in love . . . and I couldn't remember. I couldn't remember any of it. It made me feel—I don't know what—stupid? No, guilty. It made me feel as if I'd done something wrong to her. As if she'd given me some wonderful and expensive Christmas gift, and I'd lost it.

Before I could figure out what I was supposed to say to her, she gave a little ticktock wave of one hand and said, "Hi, Charlie." Her warm voice was low and uncertain, but it seemed to bring some light and heat into that empty, dusty, drafty, deeply shadowed room.

I licked the nervous dryness off my lips before I answered her. "Hey, Beth," I said as casually as I could. "It's good to see you."

Rick cleared his throat. I'd forgotten he was there. I'd forgotten all the guys were there.

"Well, uh . . ." Rick said.

"Yeah," said Miler. "We gotta . . . uh . . ."

"Right," said Josh. "We got a lot of things we have to . . . uh . . ."

"Exactly," said Rick.

They bumped into one another as they all started moving at once. They gathered up their sleeping bags and their litter—all except one bag and one flashlight. They left those for me. Then they headed quickly for the door.

Beth smiled to herself and looked down at the floor. She came into the room and stepped aside so the guys could get past her.

Josh was the last one out. Just as he was leaving, he turned back to me and said, "What we're gonna do: we're gonna go get some stuff. Stuff that'll help. I got all these good ideas for how we can start to find out . . ."

Rick grabbed his shirt collar and yanked him out of the room.

Beth and I stood silently, each avoiding the other's gaze. We listened as the guys' footsteps thumped down the stairs. We heard the door down there open and thud shut. Then we were alone.

I opened my mouth to say something, but nothing came to me. We went on standing there a long time.

Finally, Beth gave me a nervous smile. She moved past me over to the window. She set her carryall down on the floor. She put her hands in the pockets of her coat and shivered.

"It's really chilly in here."

"Yeah," I said. "The window . . ." I gestured lamely at the broken pane.

She seemed then to come toward me almost by accident, as if she was just wandering around the room, you know, and just happened to find herself standing right in front of me. Then she was close, looking up at me, her eyes on mine. She went up on tiptoe and kissed me.

It was just a quick kiss, quick and soft, but it made the warm, empty feeling flood through me again.

"Hi, Charlie," she repeated. It was almost a whisper this time.

"Hi," I just managed to say.

"I know you don't remember. But I remember."

Then, as if she had embarrassed herself, her cheeks turned red and she moved away.

"I brought you some food," she said quickly.

"Oh, hey, that's really nice."

"It's just some sandwiches and an apple. A couple of bottles of water. But I figured the guys wouldn't think of it or they'd just bring you chips or Pop-Tarts or something."

"Yeah." I gestured lamely again—this time at the empty soda bottles lying on the floor.

"You hungry?" she asked me.

I nodded. I was really touched she'd thought to bring me something. "I'm pretty much always hungry," I said.

She went back to her bag. Crouched down over it.

She pulled out a plaid blanket and handed it to me. "So we don't have to sit in all this dust."

"Right."

I spread the blanket out on the floor. She went into her carryall again, meanwhile, and brought out sandwiches and apples and grapes, all neatly stored in plastic bags, plus some bottles of water.

We sat on the blanket together. The sight of the sandwiches made my mouth water. It had been days since I'd eaten anything decent, anything that hadn't come from a vending machine. Also, I was glad to have something to do, you know, something to look at besides her, something to occupy me so I wouldn't have to think of more stuff to say.

I ripped into the first sandwich—chicken and cheese with mayo on a fresh roll. The taste of it—all the freshness of it and the flavor—was pretty shocking after so many weeks of scrounging for whatever I could find. The sandwich seemed practically to explode in my mouth and the taste traveled all through me.

"Good," I said with my mouth full. "Really good. Really."

She smiled. She sat there and watched me eat. It felt like she was practically studying my face. When I stole glances at her, I could see her eyes glistening in the daylight that came in through the window. It made me feel funny to have her look at me that way—you know, as if she had been wanting to see me for a long time and now that I was here, she couldn't take her eyes off me. It made me feel good. In fact, I had to keep from getting a stupid-looking smile on my face. I forced it down, but it kept coming back. I finally hid it with another bite of the sandwich.

"Has it been terrible?" Beth said finally.

"Has what been terrible?"

"You know, having to run away all the time. Is it really bad?"

I shrugged. It had been a long time since anyone had asked me a question like that—a question about how I was feeling. Used to be, I'd hear it every day, practically every hour. I'd wake up and my mom would say, "How'd you sleep?" I'd go to school and my friends would say, "How's it going?" At night, at dinner, my dad would say, "How was school?" Sometimes it could even feel annoying, you know—like why does everybody have to ask me questions all the time?

But when it stops, when nobody asks—when nobody cares how your day was or how you slept or how it's going for you—then you miss it, I can tell you. You miss it a lot.

So when Beth asked, I suddenly wanted to tell her everything. I wanted to try to explain to her how it felt to have everything you cared about and loved suddenly vanish. I wanted to tell her what it was like to be on the road, hunted, day and night, with nowhere you could call home. I wanted her to know what it did to you to have the world think you were evil and to wonder sometimes yourself whether you were or not.

I wanted to tell her—but I couldn't find the words.

"I don't know," I said finally. "It's kind of lonely sometimes."

She nodded. "I think it must be. Must be scary too."

I shrugged again. She was right, of course. It was scary. It was scary all the time, every minute. But I didn't like to tell her that. "I guess," I said. "I guess it's kind of scary sometimes."

"I'd be scared," she said. "I'd be scared all the time. I am scared all the time."

"You are? Why? What are you scared about?"

"I'm scared for you, Charlie," she said, in a tone of voice that suggested it had maybe been kind of a stupid question. "I mean, I try not to think about it, but I can't

151

help it. I think of you out there all alone with the police after you and I get so worried I . . ." Her eyes glistened even more. She didn't finish.

I tried to think of the right thing to say. "Don't be scared," was all I could come up with. "I mean, here I am, right? I'm okay. I'm gonna be okay."

"I know," she said hoarsely, trying to smile. "I know you are."

"I'm sorry, Beth. I'm sorry you have to worry like that."

She shook her head. "It's not your fault."

"I don't know whether it is or not."

"It's not."

"Maybe . . . but I'm sorry anyway. I'm sorry you have to worry. I'm sorry I can't be here to . . . you know, to keep you from worrying and make you feel better. And you know what I'm sorry about more than anything?"

She shook her head. She couldn't speak. She was trying too hard not to cry.

I told her, "I'm sorry I can't remember. Us, you know. I'm sorry I can't remember us."

She nodded. She managed to get the words out. "So am I. A lot."

"I try to. I try so hard. It's really frustrating. Sometimes it feels like . . . it's all still there, inside my brain, just out of reach. Like when you can't remember a word or the name of a song or something, but it's right on the tip of your tongue. It feels like that. And then sometimes . . . sometimes I have dreams. You know? Dreams about you and me. Just you and me walking together or talking or something. And then I wake up and . . . I don't know whether I was remembering something that really happened or if it was just a dream."

"That does sound frustrating."

"Yeah. Yeah, it is."

Talking to Beth was kind of an amazing thing. The way she listened to you—it made you feel like you were the only person in the world, the only thing she was interested in or really cared about. I mean, I didn't want to complain too much. Mostly I didn't want to say anything that would make her worry even more than she already did. But it sure felt good to say these things to her, to tell her about all these things I'd been keeping inside me during all the weeks when I had no one to talk to.

"It's like that with a lot of stuff," I said. "All the stuff I can't remember. A whole year—it's just gone. Not just you and me but . . . how I got arrested. My trial. I can't even remember . . ."

The words stuck in my throat. Beth reached out and touched my hand gently. "What, Charlie?"

"I can't even remember if I'm guilty or not."

"What do you mean?"

"Alex. I can't even remember if I killed him."

"Oh, Charlie." Her hand closed over mine. "Of course you didn't. I know that. We all do."

Man, I have to say: it was hard not to cry when she said that. I would've rather the Homelanders stormed into the room just then and shot me dead before I let Beth see me cry, but it was hard not to. For a long time, I couldn't say anything at all.

Finally, I forced the words out. "The police . . . The jury . . . They all think I did it."

"Well, they're wrong, that's all. They've made a terrible mistake. I'm sure they didn't mean to. They were trying to get it right, but somehow things just got mixed up."

"And now there are these people. These terrorists. They think I'm one of them."

"Oh, Charlie, you have to know that's not true."

"I want to. I want to know it, Beth. So help me, I want to know it more than anything. I mean, I'm not trying to say I'm anybody special or Superman or anything like that, but . . . I always thought I was all right. You know? I thought I was a decent guy . . ."

"You are. Of course you are. You're more than that."

"Then why do they all . . . ?" I lifted the last of the sandwich, but I didn't eat it. I couldn't. My throat felt so tight I knew I wouldn't be able to get it down. "I try to figure it out, but I can't. You know? It doesn't make any sense. If I'm really innocent, why would everyone say I was guilty? I feel like, if I could just remember what happened . . ."

"You will. You just have to keep trying. I'm sure you will."

I put the sandwich down. I reached into my fleece and brought out the papers I'd got in the library.

"It's why I came back. To see if I could piece it all together and figure it out. I mean, if I didn't kill Alex, someone else must've done it, right? The paper said it was someone he recognized, someone he knew. If it wasn't me, then who was it?"

She took the papers from me. She paged through them silently for a few moments. As she did, the tears welled in her eyes again. One tear spilled over and ran down her cheek. I could feel it—that tear. I felt it like a punch. I reached out with one finger and brushed it off her.

"Don't cry," I said.

"It was just . . . it was so awful. The trial and everything."

"You were there?"

"Every day, whenever I could be. And afterward, I'd come to your house . . . It was just getting started between us and . . . they took you away from me."

An eagerness rose in me. It shot up like a flame. "Tell me," I said to her. "Tell me . . . the whole thing. The arrest, the trial and . . . and us. Tell me about us, Beth. Please. I need to know. Tell me about us."

And she did.

CHAPTER SEVENTEEN

Love and Death

Of all the strange things that had been happening to me, I don't think anything felt quite so bizarre as having Beth tell me the story of my own life—that crucial part of it anyway, when I had both fallen in love and been convicted of murder. I had told her everything at the time, of course, so she knew pretty much the whole chain of events. And to have her telling me things about myself— really personal important things—that I didn't know was, like . . . well, it was very, very weird.

This is what she said had happened after the night Alex was murdered, after the last day I could remember.

The news of Alex's stabbing flashed through the town like lightning. Phones started ringing everywhere first thing in the morning. Everyone knew about it even before the newspaper arrived with the story on the front page.

The second I heard the news, Beth said, I knew I had to go to the police. I knew I must've been one of the last people to see Alex alive.

My dad called the police for me. Then he and I went to the station together. I guess that was the first time I met Detective Rose.

We went into an interrogation room, a small dingy room with dirty white soundproofing on the walls and a video camera hanging up in one corner of the ceiling so other policemen could watch you being questioned on a TV in another room. My dad was with me the whole time, but still, it made me nervous to be questioned by a police detective. Whenever you see people getting questioned by detectives on TV, there's always a lot of yelling and a lot of times the guy being questioned gets taken away in handcuffs. Even though it was nothing like that in real life, it was still pretty tense. Plus, Detective Rose wasn't exactly what you'd call the most relaxing person to talk to.

He was on the short side but trim and fit as if he went to the gym a lot. He was black, with a round face and a thin mustache. He had short hair and a receding hairline. His features looked like someone had pushed them flat. But the features that really caught your attention were his eyes. His eyes were cold and smart. They watched you and took in everything. Detective Rose always gave you the feeling that he knew everything you'd done and everything you were thinking.

Even then, even at the very start, I could see there were a lot of reasons for Detective Rose to be suspicious of me. I could see that he might even think I had killed Alex. Alex and I had argued—there were witnesses who had seen us and heard us. And Alex had obviously known the person who approached him in the park. Then there was the fact that Alex had died gasping out my name: "Charlie . . . Charlie . . ."

So, sure, all of that put together made me nervous. Nervous—but not scared. I wasn't scared because I knew I hadn't done anything wrong.

I told Rose what happened, the whole story about

Alex and me. He asked me questions and I answered them. When he was done, he asked me to give him the clothes I was wearing the night before. I said sure. He asked for a sample of my DNA. I said sure again. Some guy came in and took some spit out of my mouth with a cotton swab. Finally Detective Rose asked if I'd take a lie detector test and I said another sure and I did.

A couple of days later, Rose came by my house. He acted differently this time. His eyes stayed cool and watchful, but he smiled more. He talked to my father in a friendly voice.

He told my dad that there was nothing to worry about. It would be weeks before all the tests came back, the DNA and everything. But I had passed the lie detector test with flying colors and, he said, he was willing to "stake his reputation as a detective" on the fact that I hadn't killed Alex.

Well, again (this is what Beth told me that I told her), I wasn't scared, but it was a relief to be off the list of suspects.

All the same, I was still pretty down about Alex. Everyone was. We had an assembly at school to talk about him. Mr. Woodman, the principal, who usually couldn't put two sentences together without stumbling over his own tongue, suddenly became almost eloquent, talking about Alex's life and how we would never know what he could have made of it. There was no clowning around in the auditorium while he spoke, the way there usually was. Everyone just sat there, looking grim. A lot of the girls were crying.

Sometime later that week, I phoned Beth. She had given me her number and I'd said I was going to call, so I did. Originally, I'd been going to ask her out. But we talked about it and, after the murder and everything, it didn't seem right somehow to just go out to a movie or something. So we decided we would take a walk together instead and talk about things.

That Saturday, I met Beth down by the Spring River. There's a really nice path there that goes along the river and through a birch tree forest. There's a lane for bikes, but most of it is just for walking. We went in the morning before the path got crowded. In early autumn the birch leaves turn this really beautiful orange-yellow and the sun was shining through them so that they looked almost like fire against the blue of the sky. We walked under them side by side.

"It's messed up about Alex," I said.

"It's really messed up," said Beth. "It must be kind of

weird for you to be one of the last people who saw him."

"Yeah, it kind of is. I feel bad because we ended up arguing. Now I'll never get to make it good."

I told her all about what happened. I told her about the police questioning me and so on.

"I still can't believe it."

"I went by his house yesterday to visit his mother," Beth said. "I never saw anyone look like she did. She looked like she was the one who died. I mean, first her husband leaves and now . . ."

"It was nice of you to go over there."

"Alex and I got to be friends last summer. I knew he'd been having a lot of troubles since his dad left and . . . Well, the way he was acting, I couldn't go on seeing him, you know. But deep down, he was a good person. I wish we could've helped him somehow."

"Me too. I always figured he'd straighten himself out, you know. You never figure someone that young is just going to run out of time."

"Do you think they'll catch the person who did it?"

"Oh yeah. Sure they will. I mean, it's probably not that big a mystery. Alex was getting in with some bad kids at his school, getting into some bad stuff. Drinking, hanging out. I'm sure there were drugs too."

"I know there were," said Beth.

"The police probably know about all those people already. They just have to find the right one."

I sounded very sure of it, Beth told me. But, in fact, the police investigation went on for weeks and there were no suspects. And life went on too. And, after a while, people didn't talk about the murder all the time and they didn't feel sad all the time. Alex and his death sort of faded into the background.

Beth and I started walking home together after school. It still didn't feel right to date somehow, but we went to lunch a couple of times and bowling once. Then one Saturday afternoon, we went to a movie together. There were a lot of movies at the malls in town, but we didn't go to one of those. We went to a little theater on a small street near the airport. The theater was kind of run-down and the pictures that played there were months old, but it was a nice place to be sometimes because it was out of the way and you were less likely to see any of the people you knew. I guess there was something about me and Beth being together that had begun to feel kind of private at that point.

Anyway, we were sitting in the theater before the lights went down, passing a popcorn bag back and forth and just kind of staring at the advertising slide show on the screen and talking about stuff.

And Beth said, "I feel a little strange about this."

"What do you mean?" I asked her. "About going to the movies?"

"I don't know. I still think about Alex and everything. I mean, I know life goes on, but . . . do you feel like it might be wrong for us to be here?"

There was a silence. Then I said, "I feel . . ."

But before I could finish, the lights went down and the movie trailers started.

When we came outside after the movie, it was dark. We decided we would go back into town and have dinner at a place called Marie's where a lot of the kids hung out. As we were walking to our cars, I took hold of Beth's hand. It was the first time I had done that.

When we reached her car, we stopped and stood facing each other. I was looking into her eyes. Her eyes were blue, but they were a sort of pale blue with flecks of gold in them. The color reminded me of flowers.

"What were you going to say?" she asked me. "Before the movie started. I said it felt a little wrong for us to be there and you said, 'I feel . . .' and then you didn't finish. What were you going to say? Do you remember?"

"Yeah, I remember. I was going to say: I feel like nothing about you and me being together is wrong. I feel like when we're together, it's just right, like it's supposed to happen. It's weird, too, because it's not like in the movies with music playing or fireworks or—or anything that I expected. It's just like . . . I don't know, like a little click, like— You ever do jigsaw puzzles? And you find the right piece and it clicks in? It feels like that."

Beth said, "It feels like that to me too," and I kissed her.

CHAPTER EIGHTEEN

The Worst Thing Ever

The wind outside had fallen off, but, all the same, a chill drifted in through the broken window of the Ghost Mansion's parlor. Beth paused in her story. She shivered and I shivered and we both looked away.

It was kind of embarrassing, that's all—sitting there, listening to Beth describe what I said to her and how I kissed her. It was embarrassing—and it was molto weird, too, because I didn't remember any of it. I didn't remember saying that stuff about the jigsaw pieces fitting together and everything—although, I have to admit, when she told it to me, I thought it was a pretty cool thing to have said. Because, the thing was, I could feel it, even now. I could feel it was true right that second, sitting there with her.

"I bet that was nice," I said. "Kissing you for the first time. I wish I could remember what that was like."

"It was like this," she told me.

And then we didn't say anything for a while.

And for a while, Beth told me, Alex and the murder fell into the background of our lives. Just about everything did, except for us being together. Walking home together, going out together, being around each other. It was as if we had made some kind of discovery—as if we had discovered something that had been right there in front of us and yet hidden away at the same time. I guess we'd fallen in love. Which, I guess, happens a lot in the world. But it felt to us like it had never happened to anyone before. It felt like nothing that special and yet so incredibly *right* could happen any more than once in a million years.

We were together every minute we could be. We did homework together and watched TV together. We talked and talked to each other, telling each other the stories of our lives, everything we hoped to do after we got out of school and all the secret stuff we thought about that we never told anyone.

"It's like we're two different computers downloading our programs into each other," I said to her. "It's like we're becoming a two-machine network running the same software."

She laughed at me. "Only a guy would say something like that."

"Why?" I said. "What do you mean?"

"Well, it's, like, the least romantic thing I think I've ever heard. In fact, it may be the least romantic thing anybody's ever said."

I laughed too. "Come on! You think it's the least romantic thing anybody's ever said? Ever? What about, like, cabbage. Or mud. Or, Hey, Al, I dropped my cabbage in the mud."

"Even that is more romantic than comparing us to two machines with the same software."

"It's a very romantic concept."

"To a guy!"

"It's like a love song or something." I sang it to her: "You're the software that makes my computer full—and that's why I think you're so beauter-full . . ."

That made her laugh even more. Or maybe it was just my singing voice, which, I've noticed, makes a lot of people laugh.

Anyway, it seems we spent a lot of time together talking about stupid stuff like that and then laughing about it. And we would wonder to each other sometimes why anyone would ever do anything else, why everyone didn't spend all of their time just saying stupid things and laughing. It seemed like the best thing two people could possibly do.

But then we stopped. Suddenly. We stopped laughing. We stopped saying stupid things. All our happiness came crashing down around us.

It happened on a Tuesday, early morning, before school. I called Beth and told her we had to meet at our place. I told her it was important.

Our place was the path by the river, the path where we'd walked that first time together. We met there sometimes in the early morning when there were no crowds, no one except the occasional young professional getting in some biking exercise before the day began.

The autumn had gone on now and the leaves were falling. The branches of the birches were almost bare and the yellow leaves lay in the grass beside the path and blew rattling across the pavement. The weather was turning too. The sky that morning was steel gray, and there was a damp chill in the air that told you winter was coming.

Beth got to the path before me and waited. When she saw me coming, when she saw my face, she knew right away that something was really wrong.

"Charlie? Are you okay? What's the matter?" she said.

She reached out with both her hands to take my hands. But I wouldn't give them to her. I stood at a little distance with my thumbs in my pockets. I looked at her and my face was hard, she said, as if I was trying to look angry or mean. But she saw something else in my eyes.

"Look," I told her. "I don't want to hurt your feelings or anything, but we have to stop."

"Stop what?"

"Stop seeing each other. We can't see each other anymore."

"Charlie, what're you talking about? Why?"

"Well, because . . . We just should. That's the way I want it, all right? It's—I don't know—it's just getting too serious for me. After a while, we'll go to college or whatever and . . . what's the point, you know? Look, I just think it's the right thing to do. I don't feel the same way about you anymore and I—I just want to end it, that's all."

Beth stared at me a long time. She had a sick feeling in her stomach, but it wasn't what she expected. She wasn't sad, as if we were breaking up. Instead, she was afraid and she wasn't sure why.

She shook her head. She stepped closer to me, studying my face, studying my eyes.

Then she said, "You're lying to me, Charlie. I never saw you lie before, but I know it when I see it. Why are you lying to me?"

"I'm not . . ."

"Yes, you are. I know it when I see it. You're not doing this because your feelings have changed. You feel just the same . . ."

"No, I don't."

"Yes, you do, Charlie. Don't lie." I looked away from her and she knew she was right. "Tell me what's the matter."

When I looked at her again, my face was still set, still hard, but she could see the doubt in my eyes.

"Look," I told her. "It just . . . it isn't right, that's all. You and me. It's a mistake."

"Don't say that. You know that's not true."

"You're just going to get hurt, Beth. That's all I'm try-ing to tell you, all right? I just don't want you to get hurt."

"You have to tell me what's wrong."

"Look . . ." I tried again. "Look, I can't. I can't tell you. Okay? We have to end it, that's all. Can't we just leave it at that?"

"No," Beth said. "We can't. I mean, haven't you been paying attention? We don't have the right to just end this. We didn't make it and we can't end it."

"I don't even know what that means," I said sourly.

She put her hand on my arm. This time I let her. "Charlie, look at me." It seemed to her I had to force myself to meet her eyes. "Charlie, this thing happening with us—it doesn't happen to everyone. They say it does in the movies, but it doesn't. It's special. You know that, right?"

"Yeah. I know it."

"Then you know we can't just throw it away because there's some kind of trouble."

"I'm not trying to throw it away, I'm just . . . Aw, Beth." I bowed my head and dug the heels of my palms into my eyes. "I don't even know what to do."

"Just tell me what's happening."

It was a long time before I could raise my head and

look at her again. "It's the worst thing," I said. "The worst thing ever." Now all the hardness was gone from my face. Now it was me reaching out for her, taking her by the shoulders. "They're coming for me, Beth."

"Who? Who is?"

"The police. They're going to arrest me."

"Arrest you? For what?" But she already knew. "For Alex? How do you know?"

"I know. That detective . . . That detective Rose. He called my dad. They . . . they found a knife. A combat knife. It's the murder weapon and . . . Well, they say it has my fingerprints on it and my DNA. And they say there are traces of Alex's blood on my clothes."

She stared up at me. "There has to be some kind of mistake. I mean, how could that happen?"

"I don't know, I . . ." She saw my shoulders sag. I closed my eyes a moment as if I were surrendering to something inside myself. When I opened them again, Beth said, it was as if a mask had fallen away from my face. As if I had been pretending to be someone else and now I was Charlie again. I said to her, "Listen to me, Beth. All right? Listen because . . . well, because I need you to get this. I didn't kill him. Okay? No matter what happens, no matter what you hear, no matter what it looks like, I didn't kill Alex. You looked at me before and you knew I was lying. Now I need you to look at me and believe I'm telling the truth."

"I am," she said softly. "I do."

"Never stop. Okay? Never stop believing it. No matter what happens."

"I won't."

I took her into my arms and held her against me. "You were right," I said, my lips against her ear. "You were right and I was wrong. The stuff I feel for you—I didn't make it and it isn't mine to throw away. And I won't. I can't."

"I can't either. And I won't, Charlie. I promise."

"No matter what happens."

"No matter what."

When I got to school that morning, the police were waiting for me.

CHAPTER NINETEEN

An Incredibly Stupid Plan

When Beth was finished telling me about that, we sat together holding hands. As the chill air blew through the parlor window, a smell of autumn leaves came to me from outside. The smell brought a touch of memory with it. That happens a lot, I've noticed—smells bring memories and memories bring smells. For a moment, as I breathed in the scent of the fallen leaves, I felt as if I could almost recall the days Beth and I had had together. All the stuff she was telling me about—I felt it was there, in my mind, just beyond my reach. I felt if I could just concentrate hard enough, it would all come flooding back to me. But the harder I tried, the further away it seemed.

Then the smell was gone and the memory was gone and I let out a long breath and shook my head.

"What?" said Beth.

"Nothing. It doesn't matter." She was still here anyway. Beth was still here, still looking at me that way—the same way she must've looked at me on the path that day. "Why did you believe me?" I asked her suddenly. "When I told you I didn't kill Alex. I mean, the police had fingerprints, they had DNA, they had bloodstains. Why did you believe I didn't do it? I mean, maybe I'm just a really good liar."

"You probably are a good liar when you want to be," she said. "But it wasn't that. It wasn't that I believed you. It was that I knew you. I mean, we hadn't been together very long, but in some ways I knew you better than I'd ever known anyone. It was like . . . like we'd always known each other . . . like . . ."

"Like we were two computers running the same software," I said.

She smiled and I smiled.

"Right," she said. "I mean, I'm not gonna say you could never kill anyone, Charlie. You could kill someone, I think. If it was a war or something or if someone was trying to hurt someone you loved and there was no other way to stop him. I think you could kill someone then. But you couldn't murder anyone. Or maybe it's not that you couldn't—you wouldn't. You wouldn't just kill someone for no reason or because you were angry at him or anything like that. You might feel like it, but you wouldn't let yourself. It just isn't who you are."

I shook my head. "I wish I knew that."

"I wish you did too. I think you did know it once. I think you just can't remember it, that's all." She reached out and put her finger on the corner of my mouth, as if trying to push it up and get me to smile again. "It wasn't just me, you know. Rick and Josh and Miler—they all knew you were innocent. Your parents knew. Your sister knew. Your karate teacher—Mike. He came to the trial a lot. So did Mr. Sherman."

"Mr. Sherman? I always thought he hated me."

"He didn't hate you. He just disagreed with you, that's all. But he knew you weren't a murderer. He stood by you the whole time. You guys really became close."

"We did? Go figure. I guess you never know who

your friends are until there's trouble. Tell me more. Tell me about the trial."

"It was weird. It happened really fast. Everyone said so . . ."

She was about to go on, but just then there was a noise downstairs: the door opening.

Instantly, I was on my feet. I was at the door, crouched in a fighting position. I gestured to Beth to be quiet.

But the next second, I relaxed. It was the guys. I could tell just by the way they came galumphing up the stairs like elephants. After another second, I could hear their voices too.

"Don't drop it." That was Rick, trying to whisper and whispering so loudly they could've heard him in the next town over.

"Hey, do you want to carry it?" That was Miler, loud-whispering back. Then, just before they came into view on the second-floor landing, he spoke more clearly in what was possibly the worst Russian accent I've ever heard. "We are comink to find you, younk lovers. No more kissy-kissy face, da?"

I rolled my eyes. "What an idiot."

There they were. Miler first, then Rick behind him. Miler was swinging a plastic shopping bag in his hand.

Rick had what looked like a laptop computer case strapped over his shoulder.

Miler went on making kissing noises as he came toward the door. "Mwah, mwah, mwah. We are not being, I hope, interrrrrruptink anytink?"

"Aren't you supposed to be in school?" I said.

"Aren't you supposed to be in prison?"

"I'm a fugitive. What's your excuse?"

"I'm a senior. My first period is lunch. Then I have PE. Then I wave at the stats teacher for credit. Then I have my driver take me to the Savoy for afternoon tea."

"The school finally figured out they couldn't teach Miler anything," said Rick, coming up behind him. "They're just keeping him around 'cause we're used to him, like the stuffed lion at the basketball games."

They came into the parlor and set their packages down on the floor.

"Has this man been bothering you?" Miler asked Beth. She laughed.

"What's all this stuff?" I said.

Rick planted himself cross-legged on the floor in front of the laptop case. He opened it. "This," he said, "is the stuff we need for Josh's incredibly stupid plan."

"For instance, here's a cell phone with two-way

capabilities," said Miler. "Because Josh doesn't have a remote headset for his computer." He brought the phone out of the plastic bag and tried to hand it to me.

I wouldn't take it. "I can't use a cell phone. The police can trace them in about ten seconds."

"Not this one. It's not registered to you and it's disposable. Just like the drug dealers use."

"Great. If drug dealers are doing it, it must be good. Man, this really does sound like an incredibly stupid plan. What is it?"

"Voilà," said Rick—only he pronounced it Voy-la. He had set the laptop up on the floor now and pressed the Power button. The machine had obviously already been booted up and in sleep mode because it came on right away. The monitor winked on and . . .

"You gotta be kidding me," I said.

But they weren't. There on the monitor was Josh. It was a live webcam shot of him sitting behind the wheel of his mom's black Camry, driving down the road.

"Josh knew this house picks up the hot spots from the mall," said Rick. "How he knew, I have no idea, but he knew."

Miler flipped the cell phone open and spoke into it. "Calling Agent Dipstick. Calling Agent Dipstick."

On the computer monitor, Josh put his finger to his ear as if he had a headset on. It must've been a pretty small headset, though, because I couldn't see it. It must've been like one of those hearing aids you stick inside your ear.

"I hear voices," Josh said. "Must be aliens." I couldn't see his microphone either, but it must've been there because his voice came back over the two-way's speaker, loud enough for all of us to hear.

"Give me that," I said to Miler. I took the two-way from him. I knelt down in front of the laptop so I could see Josh more clearly. I spoke into the phone. "Josh, what do you think you're doing? Where are you going?"

I could see Josh on the monitor, steering the car with one hand and touching his headset with the other. I could see him glance over at the seat, blinking through his big glasses, when he talked back to me. I guess that's where the webcam was. "I'm driving to Wyatt High School," he said.

I felt a twinge inside me. Wyatt High School—that was where Alex used to go. "Why are you going there?"

"Because you can't, my friend. If you go to Wyatt High School and start asking all kinds of questions, you'll get arrested. So I'm going instead. I figured I'd start with the two kids who witnessed Alex's murder. Bobby Hernandez and Steve Hassel. They were in middle school then, but they moved up this year. I'll talk to them; you watch me on the webcam, and that way, you can tell me what questions you want to ask. Then I'll ask and you'll be able to hear the answers. I'll even be able to clip the webcam to my shirt or something so you'll be able to see who I'm talking to. Good plan, right?"

"Amazing," I said into the phone. "Only listen. There's a new plan. In this plan, you turn your car around and drive home and then go to school."

"I went to school already. I don't have another class till two. I'm a senior, remember?"

"All right, then don't go to school. Stay home and watch cartoons on television. Just don't go around asking questions about Alex's murder."

"Why not?"

My voice rose. "Because it's dangerous, Josh, that's why. I told you guys: this isn't a game. It's not a television show. There are real people really trying to hurt me. Really bad. And they'll hurt you too."

"Well, what's your plan?" said Josh.

"Well . . ."

"Weren't you going to go around asking people questions?"

"Yeah, but . . ."

"And where were you going to start?"

I had to admit it. "I was gonna start at Wyatt too, but . . ."

"So it's the same thing," said Josh. "Only I'm going to do it for you so you don't get caught."

"But . . ." I began—then nothing. I knelt there like an idiot, trying to think of an argument. Finally I said, "It's too dangerous, Josh."

"It's a lot less dangerous for me than it is for you," Josh answered right away. "In fact, it's not really that dangerous for me at all. If someone stops me or asks me what I'm doing, I'll just tell them I'm writing an article about Alex's murder for the school paper. You know, a kind of retrospective."

"But . . ." I said again. This was so frustrating. Josh was making really good arguments and I had no answer for them—but I still didn't want him out there taking the risks that were meant for me. I turned to Rick, then Miler, looking to them to help me out here.

"We had the same problem," Miler told me. "Josh's plan is incredibly stupid—but it's actually the least incredibly stupid plan any of us could think of."

I looked to Beth now, hoping she'd suggest something.

Sitting on the picnic blanket, she only lifted one shoulder in a shrug.

"This is exactly what I didn't want to happen," I said.

"Yeah, life can be like that sometimes," said Josh through the two-way.

"Josh . . ." I said through gritted teeth. I think if Beth hadn't been there, I'd have said a lot more.

"Look," said Rick. "You have to give the man credit where it's due. It really is safer for him to ask questions than it would be for you. And with all this spy stuff, at least we'll be able to keep tabs on him."

I covered the two-way with my hand so Josh couldn't hear me. "Why didn't you go?" I asked Rick. "You're twice his size."

"Yeah, but Josh actually is the editor of the school paper, so we thought his alibi would pan out. Also, it's his spy stuff."

I sighed. I uncovered the two-way. "All right," I said. "We'll try it this one time. But if you get killed, Josh, I'm gonna personally kick your butt into the middle of next Tuesday."

I could see him on the monitor, turning the steering wheel again. I could see the scenery change through the driver's window as he went around a corner.

"I'm not gonna get killed," he said. "I'll just go to the high school, chat with Hernandez and Hassel, and leave."

"No," I said. "Not them."

"Come on, Charlie," said Josh. "I'm telling you. It'll be safe."

"Yeah, all right, all right, but still—not Hernandez and Hassel. They're just witnesses. They don't really know anything; they just saw stuff. And they already told what they saw to the police. Plus, they testified and talked to the media too. We're not gonna find out anything from them we can't find out by reading the newspapers."

Rick made a face at Miler. Miler made a face at Rick.

Coming over the two-way, Josh said, "I didn't think of that. That's pretty smart. All right. Who should I talk to then?"

I'd already thought of that—I'd thought of it a few days ago when I was planning to come here.

"The night Alex died, he was hanging out with two friends at the Eastfield Mall. I know because they came up to me and gave me a hard time about talking to Beth. They acted like they were going to start a fight with me, and they only stopped when Alex called them off."

"Right. You said all that at your trial," said Josh. "And those two guys testified too."

"I know. I have a newspaper story with their names in it. The thing is, they were Alex's friends. They knew what he was into, who he was talking to. They knew what he was planning to do that night."

Rick spoke up, sitting cross-legged next to me. "Wouldn't the police have talked to them, too, same as the witnesses?"

"Yeah," I told him. "But maybe they didn't ask them the right questions or maybe they didn't follow up on the ones they did ask. See, once they found the knife and the DNA and everything, they were sure I was the one who did it. Maybe they figured there wasn't any need to find out anything else after that. It's possible they got side-tracked, that's all."

Once again, Rick and Miler exchanged a look. Miler shrugged. Then Rick shrugged. "I guess it's possible," he said.

Josh's voice came over the two-way. "Well, I guess we're going to find out. Here we are."

We all turned back to the laptop again. On the monitor, Josh was spinning the steering wheel to guide the Camry into a parking space. Through his window, I could see parts of the high school going by in the background.

"All right," said Josh. "I guess this is it."

He sounded excited, as if this was an adventure. That worried me. He should've sounded scared, as if this was dangerous. Because it was dangerous. I mean, I was scared, and I wasn't even there.

"You got the names of those kids?" he said.

Beth handed me my little sheaf of news stories. I paged through them until I found the names.

"Paul Hunt and Frederick Brown."

CHAPTER TWENTY

Hunt

Wyatt High School is a pretty rough place. It's in a run-down section of town—the section Alex had to move to after his dad left. A lot of the kids who go to Wyatt have really hard lives: no fathers, not enough money, sometimes violent homes and stuff like that. They have a big problem at the school with booze and drugs. They also have a big problem with gangs—a lot of the kids belong to them. A couple of times, the police have had to rush to the school to break up fights on the field out back. These weren't just schoolyard punch-outs either, they were full-scale melees with knives and baseball bats and so on.

The idea of skinny, pale-faced, geeky Josh with his big glasses and his goofy smile wandering around asking these kids questions didn't make me feel any better about the situation. But there he was.

Josh spent some time fumbling around in the car getting his spy gear all hooked up. He was wearing slacks and a checked button-down shirt with a tan windbreaker over it: sort of the official geek uniform. He hooked his webcam up to the collar of his windbreaker. We couldn't see it, but he told us it was made to look like some kind of medallion so it wouldn't be so noticeable. He hooked his microphone up to his shirt collar near his mouth, under the windbreaker so no one could see it. Then he pulled a watch cap down over his head. It was a little warm to be wearing a watch cap, but it hid the earpiece. Finally, he strapped a laptop case over his shoulder. He had to carry it with him so the webcam and mike would work.

Now he stepped out of the car.

In the empty parlor of the Ghost Mansion, with the cool air blowing in from the graveyard through the broken window, Beth and Rick and Miler and I crowded around our own laptop, watching the monitor intently.

We couldn't see Josh, but we could see whatever was in front of him. At first, as he climbed out of his mom's Camry, the scenery swung around wildly in this kind of sickening way. We caught tilted, pixilated glimpses of the parking lot and the school's grassy backfield and the school building itself—which was one of those old-fashioned brick buildings with the clock tower and the white cupola up top.

Then Josh started walking and the picture steadied. It still kind of bumped around with his footsteps, but at least it didn't swing back and forth anymore.

Josh narrated into the microphone under his breath. "Here I go, moving across the field . . ."

"We can see that, Josh," said Miler. "You're wearing a camera on your shirt."

Josh ignored him. "I'm looking around now to find someone I can talk to . . ."

"Dork," muttered Miler with a sigh.

As Josh turned to look this way and that, we got a pretty fair view of the field. We could see that even now, about an hour before lunchtime, there were a lot of kids out there. I guess they were mostly seniors who didn't have many classes to go to. Some of them were playing basketball on the paved court to one side of the field.

Some of them were kicking a soccer ball around in the grass. A lot of them were just standing in clusters, talking and sneaking cigarettes and looking shiftily this way and that as if they wanted to make sure there were no teachers nearby. I knew they weren't allowed to wear gang colors at school, but I'm pretty sure some of these kids were gangsters all the same.

"Okay," whispered Josh into his microphone. "There's someone . . ."

On the monitor now, we saw a small cluster of kids coming closer and closer as Josh approached them. They were standing right at the edge of the field, near one corner of the parking lot. There were four of them, four guys standing together. They didn't exactly look like Mr. Friendly and his Happyface Pals. They were big, dressed in denim, one dude with cut-off sleeves so you could see his enormous arm muscles. Two of them were smoking cigarettes. None of them were smiling. Over the two-way, we could hear them talking in low voices, almost grunts. They would nod and frown and steal a look around and talk some more, as if they were sharing secrets.

Beth, Rick, Miler, and I all looked at one another. We were all thinking the same thing: this was not a good idea.

"Josh," I said into the two-way. "I don't think you should . . ."

"Hi, guys!" Josh greeted these thugs in his squeaky, goofy voice. "I was wondering if you could help me out!"

The guy with the big muscular arms looked at Josh. It was the way you might look at a spider when you were thinking, *Look at that disgusting little thing. I'm gonna step on it.* He didn't say anything. So Josh just plunged right on.

"I'm looking for a couple of guys I need to talk to for an article for my school paper. Their names are Paul Hunt and Frederick Brown. Any idea where I might find them?"

Beth and the guys and I stared at the laptop monitor. I think all four of us were holding our breath.

The guy with the big arms ran his eyes up and down Josh as if wondering just what kind of spider he might be. But the next minute, he kind of gestured with his head, giving it a little move that pointed across the field. The way he did it—it was like he thought Josh ought to be crushed to a green pulp, but he just couldn't be bothered to take the trouble.

Josh turned and followed the gesture. As he did, his camera swung around, and for a second I had a look in the direction the big-armed guy was pointing. Right away, I spotted one of the thugs who had approached me that night with Alex in the Eastfield Mall.

"Josh, there he is!" I said into the two-way.

"Where?" said Josh.

"What?" said the guy with the muscular arms.

"Oh," said Josh. "Uh, nothing."

"Just thank the nice man and move away, Josh," I said. "I'll guide you to the guy."

"Right," said Josh. And then to Mr. Big Arms, he said, "Hey, thanks a lot, dude."

Big Arms made another gesture with his chin, which I guess meant either *You're welcome* or *Get away from me, spider, before I change my mind and kill you.* But whatever it meant, Josh gave him a jolly, finger-waggling wave and moved off across the field.

"He is so gonna die," said Rick.

"Ssh," said Beth, afraid Josh might hear him.

"I'm just saying," said Rick.

Josh's breathless whisper came over the two-way. "Okay. I'm on the move again. Where is this guy?"

I peered into the monitor, searching. "Turn more to the left," I said. "Wait, turn back a little. There he is. You're heading right for him."

He was standing across the field. I didn't know if he was Hunt or Brown, since they hadn't introduced themselves when they were trying to bully me in the mall parking lot. At the time, I just thought of him as Crewcut Guy because he'd had his blond hair cut to a nub on his head. He was built like a low brick wall, short and thick and powerful. He was wearing a black jacket and black jeans.

Everyone else in the field was gathered in clusters with friends, but Crewcut Guy was alone. He was leaning against a diamond-link fence at the edge of the field. He had his thumbs hooked in his pockets and one of his legs bent back so his foot rested against the fence. His eyes were narrowed and his gaze moved slowly around the field, taking everything in. He reminded me of a gunfighter in an old cowboy movie, waiting for the shooting to start.

The picture of him on the laptop monitor bounced up and down as Josh approached him.

"If he didn't walk like such a geek, we could see something," muttered Rick.

"I'm starting to get motion sickness," said Miler.

"You guys are so mean," said Beth. "I thought Josh was your friend."

"We let him live, don't we?" said Rick and Miler at the same time.

Then we all fell silent again, so that the only noise in the empty parlor was Josh's panting breaths coming through the two-way speaker and the sound of his laptop slapping against his side.

Crewcut Guy got larger and larger on the monitor as Josh drew near.

"That him?" Josh muttered.

"Yeah," I told him. "Be careful, Josh. He's not as nice as he looks."

"He doesn't look very nice."

"Right."

"Oh. I get it. Yikes."

Now Crewcut Guy nearly filled the screen. He turned and looked directly at us through his squinty eyes as he noticed Josh coming toward him.

"Hi!" We heard Josh's voice cracking over the two-way speaker. "You wouldn't happen to be Paul Hunt or Frederick Brown, would you?"

"Hunt," he grunted. "What're you looking for?"

"Well, I'm doing a story for my school newspaper . . ."

The look on Hunt's face changed. He looked around, as if he thought someone was pulling a not-very-funny practical joke on him, as if he expected to find a group of his friends watching from a distance and laughing at him. The narrowed stare returned to Josh, coming straight at us on the laptop screen. "Say what?"

"I'm doing a story . . ."

"You up for something or not?"

"Yeah," said Josh. "I'm up to talk to you for a couple of minutes for my school newspaper."

Next to me, Rick rolled his eyes. Miler put his head in his hands.

"Josh, you idiot, he means drugs," I said into the two-way.

"Drugs?" said Josh.

"What do you need?" said Hunt.

"No, I didn't mean you," said Josh.

"Say what?" said Hunt. "Hey, what is this?"

"I'm doing a story for my school newspaper. It's about the murder of Alex Hauser."

Now, once again, Hunt's expression changed. When Josh mentioned Alex's name, he seemed to grow both wary and interested.

"What're you talking about? What kind of a story?"

"A retrospective," said Josh.

Hunt said, "Oh. Yeah," and he nodded. But even on

the laptop monitor, I could see that he didn't know what the word *retrospective* meant.

"We're just gonna talk about, you know, like, where the case stands now and so on."

Hunt gave an elaborate shrug—like someone pretending he wasn't interested when he really was. He brought out a cigarette and shot the filter between his lips. "What's to talk about? They got the guy, right? He and Alex fought over some piece they both wanted."

"Oh, nice," said Beth. "I'm a 'piece' now."

I held my finger to my lips.

"Ask him if he believes they got the right guy," I said into the two-way.

"Do you believe they got the right guy?" said Josh.

Hunt clicked open a big metal lighter and torched his cigarette. He shrugged again. "Sure. Why not? I met him. He was a real . . ." Well, I won't write what he called me. It's not the sort of thing I'm planning to put on my résumé— if I live to have a résumé.

All this time, I was watching Hunt's face. I could tell a lot about him just by looking at him. He had this kind of swaggering, belligerent attitude as if he was a big shot, really tough and important. But when you watched his eyes, they looked nervous, as if down deep he really felt small and insecure and afraid. I think those things go together a lot, you know? Swaggering around and secretly feeling scared. I think people act big when they feel small.

Anyway, it gave me an idea. I murmured into the two-way. "Josh, I think we gotta flatter this guy. Act like we think he's important. He's insecure—he'll fall for that. Tell him the reason you want to interview him is because you think he has real inside knowledge of the case. Use the word *interview*. Like it's some big deal. He'll like that."

We kidded Josh a lot, but there was no question he was smart. He understood exactly what I wanted. His camera went down for a moment, and we could see his hands. We saw him take a narrow pad and pen out of his coat pocket, just like a real reporter might use. "Listen, I know you're a very busy person—everyone talks about how important you are around here—so I'm really grateful you consented to this interview."

Perfect. You could see the flattery working right away. Hunt shifted his shoulders almost as if Josh had massaged them.

"Yeah," he said with this sort of haughty frown. "Yeah. Sure. I consent."

"See, the thing is, when I was researching the case, it was pretty obvious that you were the guy with the most inside knowledge."

"That's great, Josh," I said. "Now ask him if he thinks there was any other reason someone might've killed Alex. Besides the piece, I mean."

Beth leaned over and punched my shoulder. I had to grit my teeth to keep from letting out a yelp into the two-way. She had a pretty good punch for a girl.

Over the two-way speaker, I heard Josh repeating the question, really laying the flattery on thick, making it sound as if Hunt were some expert on criminology or something.

"In your considered opinion, judging Alex Hauser's psychology and all the other aspects of the crime, do you think it possible the police overlooked some other of his activities that might've led to the murder?"

Hunt preened and shifted his shoulders some more, feeling important. Josh had him now. Hunt wanted to show him what an expert he was. He wagged his cigarette at Josh as if giving him a lecture. "Well, you know, I'll tell you something. Not everybody understood Alex the way I did. He was a very deep guy."

"Really? Deep, huh."

As Josh pretended to take notes, the camera went up and down. Watching in the parlor, we could see Hunt's face and then the pad where Josh was scribbling stuff and then Hunt's face again.

"Oh yeah," said Hunt. "A real deep thinker type. You look around here . . ." Hunt gestured at the playing field. "Most of these guys, they wouldn't know an idea if it jumped out of the ground and bit them. They go around doing stuff until they get arrested or get out of town. But Alex was smart, you know. He wasn't into gangs or any really heavy drugs or anything like that. He knew where the real action in town was. That's what he was after."

"Ask him . . ." I started to say.

But Josh was already there. "What do you mean, 'the real action'?"

Now Hunt had been totally sucked in. He was really proud of his inside knowledge, really eager to show it off to Josh. He took a quick hit of his cigarette every time he spoke. He seemed to think this made him look smarter. "See, here's the thing. A person like you, you might look at a town like Spring Hill and think it's a pretty regular, straight-arrow place. But people like me and Alex, we see past the surface, you understand what

I'm saying? We know things aren't always what they seem."

"I'm not sure I understand, Mr. Hunt. Could you explain that?"

"Mr. Hunt!" Miler laughed. "Go, Josh."

"Well," Mr. Hunt explained in a ridiculously lofty tone, "you look around this town, if you don't have inside knowledge like me, you see guys walking down the street, you might think they're upstanding citizens. But the truth is: you never really know what business someone is into. I mean, the kids around here, they may do some small-time stuff. But if you want the really dirty business—the stuff where the real money is—you gotta go to the people who look clean and respectable. They're the ones pulling the strings."

"Ah," said Josh. "I see."

"Alex wasn't wasting his time doing business around here with high school kids. No way."

"You mean, he was doing business with adults?"

"Oh yeah. And you can quote me on that."

"Did you tell the police any of this?" Josh asked.

Hunt shrugged. He took a long, thoughtful drag on his cigarette. The smoke unfolded from his mouth as he talked. "I told the police what they needed to know to put that West kid in the slammer. I'm not exactly what you would call the policemen's friend, if you know what I mean."

"Right, right. Of course not."

"Maybe you shouldn't quote that."

"I won't. Anything you say."

"Ask him who, Josh," I said into the two-way. "Who was Alex doing business with? Was he doing business the night he died?"

"Who—," Josh started.

"No, wait," I said. "Make it sound like you think he doesn't know. Say something like . . ."

"I got it," Josh told me.

"Say what?" said Hunt.

"Oh . . . uh, I got what you're saying. But these people, these adults, Alex was hanging out with—I mean, that's not something he would share with you, was it? I mean, he couldn't trust just anyone with information like that."

"Nice," I murmured. Josh was good at this.

Hunt reacted just like I thought he would. "Hey, are you kidding me? Alex and I were like this . . ." He held up the two fingers holding his cigarette, squeezing them close together around the filter to show what great friends he and Alex were. "I mean, he couldn't always tell me things until they were all set up, you know, but I knew a lot, that's for sure—a lot more than people might think."

"Well, give me . . . just so my readers can get the gist here. Give me a for-instance."

"Well, like, for instance—here's something nobody knows but me practically—well, me and Brownie maybe. That night Alex died, we didn't go to the mall that night just to meet with the West character. I mean, we knew he would be there, we knew we were gonna give him a hard time. But after that, Alex was supposed to go in and have some kind of secret get-together with the teacher. This was very important, very secret stuff we weren't supposed to tell anyone. Alex was very clear about that. That's why we never told the police. We didn't know if we'd be stepping on important toes, if you see what I mean. You don't want to start trouble with the kind of people Alex knew."

"Wait, okay, go back a minute," said Josh. "The night he was killed, Alex went to the mall to see a teacher? What teacher?"

"The karate guy. What was his name? Mike."

"Mike?" I whispered. Rick and Miler and Beth all looked at me. I shook my head like a dog throwing off water, trying to clear my thoughts. Why would Alex have been arranging a secret meeting with Sensei Mike? What kind of "business" could they have been up to? And what, if anything, did it have to do with Alex getting killed?

I brought the two-way to my mouth, about to tell Josh to start asking more questions.

But just then, Hunt's image on the laptop monitor jumped violently.

Josh's voice came loudly over the two-way: "Ow!"

Now there were other voices. "Hey."

"Dude."

"Hunt."

"Who's this punk?"

Josh turned—the camera on his jacket turned—and there, in the Ghost Mansion parlor, Beth and Rick and Miler and I saw a nasty-looking face—and then another face just as nasty—and then a third face, even nastier still—staring at us through the monitor.

Josh, suddenly, was surrounded by thugs.

CHAPTER TWENTY-ONE

Fighting by Remote Control

"Uh-oh," said Rick. "This isn't good."

He was right. It wasn't. In fact, it was exactly what I'd been afraid of. It was one of the two or three hundred things I'd been afraid of, anyway.

For a few minutes there, I'd been so wrapped up in helping Josh question Hunt that I'd forgotten where he was, his surroundings. All those punks and gangsters on every side of him: they had slipped my mind. Now here they were—up close—and they didn't look happy.

"What's going on?" said one of them.

I recognized him as soon as Josh turned to him, as soon as the webcam brought his face onto the monitor. It was Frederick Brown, the other guy who'd been at the Eastfield Mall that long-ago day. He had dark skin and jet-black hair and a sort of slickly handsome face, like a guy in a cheap magazine ad. He was bigger than he was when I'd seen him last, bulked-up as if he'd been lifting weights. He had his hands jammed deep in the pockets of his dark blue track jacket, his shoulders hunched aggressively.

"You doing business here or you standing around blabbering?" he asked Hunt.

The camera swung back to Hunt. Hunt flipped his cigarette into the dirt. He felt guilty—I could see it in his eyes—as if he'd been caught doing something wrong. He was supposed to be dealing drugs and instead Josh had gotten him talking. It was as if the flattery Josh had used on him had hypnotized him, but now the arrival of his friends had awakened him from his trance.

He put his hands in his pockets and gave a guilty shrug. "What? We're just talking, Brownie."

"Talking?" This was Brown again. "That what I sent you over here to do? Talk?"

"And who's this punk?" said one of the other thugs.

"What are you talking to him about?" Josh looked at him and we saw on the monitor that he was pushing at Josh's laptop case, looking it over as if it might be something threatening—a bomb or something. If these guys found out Josh was wired, was broadcasting sound and pictures somewhere, he'd be toast. There wouldn't even be enough left of him to be toast. He'd be something you could spread on toast.

I guess Rick was thinking the same thing. "This is bad," he said. "Tell him to get out, Charlie."

"Josh, get out," I said into the two-way.

Josh's answer came back in a kind of singsong under his breath. "No can do that," the song went.

"You say something?" Brown asked him.

"Who, me?" said Josh.

"No, I'm talking to myself."

The other thugs laughed as if this was the funniest thing ever. Obviously Brown was the man in charge around here.

"Talking to yourself," said Josh with his squeaky-geeky laugh. We could hear on the two-way how scared he was. "Talking to yourself. That's good. That's funny. Talking to your—"

"Shut up," said Brown.

"Right."

Hunt stepped in in Josh's defense—in his own defense, really. "No, hey, Brownie. He's just doing a what-do-you-call-it, a retro . . ."

"Retrospective," said Josh helpfully.

"Yeah, retrospective. For a newspaper. I consented to an interview."

"That right?" said Brown. "You consented to an interview? With a newspaper."

"Yeah. Consented."

"Without talking to me."

"Uh . . . well . . . I mean, yeah, hey . . ." I could see Hunt's mind working, looking for an excuse. I could see him beginning to realize that he'd been had, that Josh had used flattery to rope him into this so-called interview.

"Say thanks a lot and good-bye, Josh," I said into the two-way.

"Well," Josh said to the thugs. "This has just been great, really . . ."

Brown ignored him, kept pressing Hunt. "And what's this interview about?"

". . . it's been terrific to talk to you all," Josh went on. "I hope we can keep in touch. Maybe have lunch."

The monitor was suddenly filled with Brown's hand

and then the scene shook violently as Brown shoved Josh in the chest.

"Didn't I tell you to shut up?"

"Oh, right," said Josh. "You did. It slipped my mind. Sorry."

"Charlie," said Beth. "If they find all his equipment— the webcam and microphone and everything—they're going to think he's spying on them for the police. They could really hurt him."

I nodded. I was already trying to think of a way out, but I could hardly get my thoughts organized. I was too busy cursing myself for being an idiot. Why had I let Josh do this? I had known what might happen . . .

"Josh," I said again. "You've got to get out of there."

Josh sang under his breath, "I know that, but ho-ow?" Then he pretended to be clearing his throat so the thugs wouldn't hear him.

"It was like I said," Hunt was explaining to Brown now. "The retro thing. We were talking about Alex. About how he got killed."

"Oh yeah?" said Brown. "About Alex, huh?"

Hunt shrugged guiltily again. He looked at Josh. Now that he was beginning to understand how Josh had suckered him, he was getting angry at him, hoping to put the blame off on him. "Hey, he's just some punk. It's no big deal."

"That right?" said Brown to Josh. "You just some punk?" Josh faced him and we saw Brown's slickly handsome face leaning in toward him. "That why you come around here asking questions?"

"Charlie," said Beth. "You've got to get him out of there now."

I took a breath and tried to clear my head. I asked myself: What would I do if I was the one standing there instead of Josh? Sometimes, in karate group classes, Sensei Mike would teach us tricks about situations like this, about how to fight when you're outnumbered. He would have a group of us gang up on one of the other students and then shout instructions about what to do. The main thing, I remembered, was you had to move in ways that forced your opponents to cut one another off, try to get them in an I formation so that only one of them had a good shot at you at any given time. Most of all, you had to avoid getting cornered or surrounded—the way Josh was now.

But even if I could help Josh maneuver himself out of the middle of the pack, what then? He was no fighter. And if he just tried to run for it, they'd take him down like a pack of dogs on a deer.

"Josh," I said. "Are there any adults there? Any teach- ers—anyone in charge who might give you a hand if you screamed for help?"

"That's no good," said Miler. "If a teacher starts ques- tioning him, they may figure out he's working for you. Then you'd have the cops on your trail again."

I knew that—but what could I do? I wasn't going to let Josh get his arms broken just to save myself.

The scene on the monitor shifted back and forth slightly as Josh tried to steal a glance at the schoolyard, as he tried to seek out someone in charge who could help him. All I saw were glimpses of kids clustered together.

"Hey!" Brown's voice came sharply over the two-way speaker. "I'm talking to you. Why are you asking ques- tions? Are you just some punk?" His threatening features filled the screen again.

"Am I a punk? That's your question?" Josh's voice broke in fear. "Well, I'm not sure how to answer that actu- ally. I suppose you could say I was a punk. On the other hand, you might say . . ."

Rick, Miler, Beth, and I all started backward as Brown shoved Josh in the chest again. It was as if his hand had come right through the monitor and shoved us at the same time.

"You trying to be funny now?" said Brown.

"Hey, Josh," I said. "If I tell you how, you think you could get up the nerve to drop this guy?"

"Drop him?" Josh squeaked.

"What?" said Brown. "What did you say?"

"Nothing."

"'Nothing' doesn't cut it. Answer my question, punk. What are you doing interviews around here for?"

"It's for my school—my school newspaper . . ."

"He's too scared to hit him," said Rick.

"And if he misses, this thug'll kill him," Miler added.

"And if he doesn't miss, the other thugs'll kill him," said Beth.

"Maybe. Maybe if I can get him to do it just right . . ." I murmured, still trying to think. Then I spoke into the two-way. "Josh, listen. Keep talking to him, say whatever you have to, say anything, but turn to your left and right while you talk so I can see exactly where these guys are standing."

Josh started babbling, "Well, let me try to answer your question as clearly as I can, okay? You see, as your colleague Mr. Hunt was saying, we're doing a retrospective on the change in attitudes that arise in a community when certain homicidal events cause an alteration . . ."

At the same time he babbled, he turned this way and that and I got a quick look at the positions of the other thugs, how they'd surrounded him.

"All right," I said, "keep talking, Josh, but listen to me very carefully and do exactly what I tell you to do . . ."

As Josh turned his attention to me, he had to talk without thinking and his babbling became even more nonsensical.

"Whereas several parties in the original configuration might have differentiated between one form of confluence and another . . ."

Rick put his head in his hand. "Dude's gonna die."

I murmured fast into the two-way. "When I say *go*, I want you to say a friendly good-bye and just stroll past this guy, walk past him to your right. Your right, Josh."

"Of course, I can totally understand if your consternation makes it appear to you that that situation is no longer viable as a subject . . ." Josh was saying.

"When you do that," I said, "the punk is going to grab your left elbow with his left hand. When that happens, you gotta move fast. Bring your left hand up and grab his elbow. Then swing around behind him and with all the strength you have, shove him in the shoulder so that he goes flying into Hunt. It'll make sense when you do it. Then run to your left—to your left, Josh, understand? Don't look back and don't stop running till you're in your car."

As Josh kept babbling, I heard—I guess we all heard—a new note of hysterical terror enter his voice. "Now of course you realize any attempt on my part to do anything of the nature you describe will result in my untimely evisceration . . ." The idea of grabbing this guy Brown and shoving him was clearly amping his fear to the max.

Up to now, Brown had been peering at Josh through narrowed eyes, pretending to understand what Josh was saying. I think maybe he was afraid if he admitted he didn't comprehend word one, he would look stupid in front of his friends. But now, his gaze shifted. His eyes grew even narrower. He wasn't looking at Josh at all anymore. He was looking at us, directly at us through the monitor.

"He sees the webcam," said Rick.

I felt a fresh burst of fear go through me.

"Hey," Brown said, cutting through Josh's palaver. His finger pointed at us through the monitor. "What's this here?"

"Oh no," said Beth.

"All right, Josh, this is it," I said into the two-way. "Do it now! Say good-bye and move past him to your right. Do it!"

"And with that," said Josh, his voice so high with fear he sounded like a cartoon mouse, "I must be off. I bid you all a fond farewell."

"What?" said Brown.

"To your right," I said into the two-way.

The scene started jogging around as Josh started moving. I got one glimpse of the surprised look on Brown's face as Josh tried to walk right past him.

"Hey, where do you think you're going?" he said.

I couldn't see it, but I had to hope he was reaching out now, grabbing Josh's elbow with his hand as I'd said he would.

"Now, Josh. Use the arm he's grabbing. Bring the hand up, grab his elbow, and swing your whole body around behind him. Shove his shoulder! Do it!"

"Me?" said Josh.

"Yeah, you!" said Brown.

"Do it!" I barked into the two-way.

"Do it, Josh!" said Beth.

"Come on!" said Rick and Miler at once.

And, to our complete amazement, Josh actually did it.

We saw a blur. He was spinning. If he had Brown's arm in his grip, he'd be able to get around behind him. And yes, there was Brown's back on the monitor. And there was Josh's hand on his shoulder, shoving him. At the same time, Josh let out what I guess was supposed to be a karate yell, but it sounded more like the shriek of a four-year-old girl running through a sprinkler.

"Eeeeeeeeeee!"

In a blurred jumble of images, I saw the startled Brown stumble forward into the equally startled Hunt. Hunt automatically reached up to catch him, but Brown went into him with such force that they both staggered backward. Then Hunt tripped and went over, carrying Brown with him so that both fell to the ground.

"Run! To your left, Josh!" I shouted. "Run to your left and don't look back!"

And that was all I could see—all any of us could see on the monitor as Josh took off as fast as he could and the picture became a jumping blur of grass and pavement and buildings all leaping around to the tune of Josh's hectic, squeaking, panting breaths.

"Oh, run, Josh!" Beth shouted at the screen, as if he needed the advice.

My hope was that when Brown and Hunt went over—when Josh cut around behind them by running to his left—their fallen forms would block the path of the other thugs, if only for a moment, giving Josh the head start he needed to make his getaway. That—and the absolute shock of being attacked by a geek like Josh—might give him just enough time to get to his car.

So far, it seemed to be working. Because now, the jouncing, blurred, crazy scene was all pavement and cars.

"He's in the parking lot!" said Miler.

But at the same moment, under the sound of Josh's breathing, we could hear grunts and footsteps growing louder behind him. The thugs had gotten out of their traffic jam. They were chasing him. And by the sound of it, they were closing in fast.

"Don't look back," I barked into the two-way.

"There's the Camry!" Rick shouted.

"Come on, Josh, come on!" Miler shouted at the screen, pumping his fist.

The black car loomed large on the monitor until it filled the screen. Over the sound of Josh's breathless gasps, we heard the beep of the door unlocking. Josh must've managed to press the button on his key as he ran.

Then we heard a thud and the screen went blank. Josh had crashed right into the side of the car. But the next moment, we saw his hands scrabbling at the door handle.

"Come on!" said Miler again.

"Hurry!" said Beth.

The door came open. We saw the inside of the car. Josh got in. We heard the car door slam.

"Yes!" said Rick.

"Lock the doors!" I shouted.

We saw the dashboard as Josh jammed his key into the ignition. We saw the windshield as he faced forward and put the car in gear.

Then Beth let out a scream that nearly made me jump through the ceiling.

One of the thugs had thrown himself onto the hood of the car, his face pressed against the windshield—and pressed terrifyingly close on our laptop screen.

Josh also let out a scream.

"Go, go, go!" I shouted.

We lost sight of the windshield as Josh turned in his seat—he had to reverse to get out of the parking space. We heard the screech of tires.

When Josh turned back, the thug on the windshield was gone—no, wait, there he was, thrown off the car by the sudden motion, spilled onto the pavement and rolling over and over.

We saw the other thugs now—Brown and Hunt and one other. They were trying to block Josh's path, trying to stand in front of the car so he'd have to stop or else run them over.

But Josh hit the gas and spun the wheel hard and we saw the thugs disappear from view as the Camry swung sharply around before they could seal it off completely.

Josh let out a wild—and kind of stupid-sounding—shriek and hit the gas. The tires shrieked back at him once more and the car shot forward.

Our faces tense, our fists clenched, we all leaned toward the monitor, eagerly staring at the images there. We saw the parking lot exit. We saw the street. We saw the scenery blur as the car went into its turn.

Josh was out. He was away.

"Yay! Yay! Yay!" we heard him screaming.

I slumped there on the floor, so relieved. I covered my eyes with my hand. I heard Beth and Rick and Miler groaning and sighing with relief all around me.

"Did you see that?" Josh shouted in a cracking voice. "Did you see what I did? Did you see me take them! I took them all! Hahahahahaha!"

I looked up, shaking my head in wonder.

Miler reached over and squeezed my arm. "Nice going, Charlie."

"Yeah, good one, West," said Rick.

I looked at Beth and she looked back at me with her eyes shining—which was somehow better than anything.

"Did you guys see that?" Josh was still screaming. "That was, like . . . it was like kung fu or Jackie Chan or something. Did you see that? *Pow! Ha! Wha!* They went over like bowling pins. Were you watching that?"

Miler laughed. "You gotta love him. He is such a moron."

I finally calmed down enough to be able to talk again. I lifted the two-way to my lips.

"We saw it, Josh."

"Did you see it? Was I monster or what?"

"You were monster, pal."

"I was monster. Wasn't I? I was Batman practically."

"Yeah," I said. "You practically were. Now get on back here, all right? And by the way, if you ever try anything like that again, so help me I will break every single bone in your body."

I snapped the two-way shut. I handed it to Miler.

"That's it," I told him—told all of them. "No more."

CHAPTER TWENTY-TWO

Nightfall

I stood at the window of the Ghost Mansion parlor. I gazed out through the gap between the last shards of glass, down at the gravestones under the trees. A chill wind blew and the leaves tumbled past the headstones. The statue of the cowled, mourning woman sent its eerie stare out over the scene.

My friends' voices came from behind me. Josh was still reliving his adventure. "Did you see that?" he asked again and again. Beth, of course, was really nice about it.

She kept telling Josh how wonderful he'd been and what a good fighter he was and how scared he must've been and how much courage it took to do what he did.

Rick and Miler took a slightly different approach.

"You are such an idiot," Rick explained to him. "If there was any justice in the world, you would be so incredibly dead by now."

"Plus, you scrim lak wooman," said Miler in his ridiculous Russian accent. "'Eeeeee.' I speet on you. *Ptui.*"

"You guys are so mean," said Beth.

I gazed out the window and watched as the light in the cemetery shifted, the sun angling overhead as afternoon came on.

Finally, I turned around and faced them. Rick was sitting on a sleeping bag, his back against the wall, one leg stretched out, the other bent so he could rest his arm across the knee. Miler lay on his back on Beth's blanket, his hands behind his head, as if he were outdoors at a picnic watching the clouds roll by above.

Josh sat Indian-style with his legs crossed, his hands moving as he described his harrowing escape.

Beth was kneeling on the blanket. She was loading what little was left of the lunch she'd brought me back into her carryall.

In a powerful burst of feeling, it came to me again how glad I was to have them here, how glad I was to see them after being on the run for so long, after being alone for so long. I'd never realized before how much my friends meant to me. I never knew how wonderful my life was until I lost it.

"Listen," I said. The word came out hoarsely. I could feel the old loneliness and sadness coming over me again, like clouds gathering.

Josh was still gabbing away. "I mean, you should've seen the look on their faces. This one guy? He looked like . . ."

"Hey, guys," I said, forcing myself to raise my voice. "Listen."

Josh's words trailed off. He and the others looked up at me.

I licked my dry lips. "You've got to go now," I told them. "You've got to. You can't stay here anymore."

For a long second, no one answered. They just sat there, staring at me, as if they hadn't heard.

"You mean, like, take off for a while, let you get some sleep?" Miler said then.

"No. I mean, like, go. Like get out of here. Leave me alone and let me do what I came here to do."

Another silence. It was as if they were a long way off and it was taking awhile for my words to reach them.

"But . . . that's all we want," said Rick. "That's why we came here—to help you do that."

"I know," I said. "But you can't. It's too dangerous. You saw what just happened."

"But . . ."

"No, listen to me, Rick. Either you go or I have to. I can't do this while I'm worrying about one of you guys getting hurt."

"Hey, that's stupid—," Rick began.

But Beth said, "No. Charlie's right." We all turned to listen to her. Beth was like that. Whenever she talked, everyone always stopped to listen. "Josh got away today, but it could've been worse. It could've been a lot worse. He might've gotten hurt. Or he might've alerted the police to Charlie. The police could be following any one of us. They know who Charlie's friends are. The bad guys probably know too. We could lead them right to him. I know we're trying to help, but we're really just making things more dangerous."

I nodded. That was exactly what I was thinking—and now that Beth said it, I knew it was right. My heart felt like it weighed a ton.

"So what are you saying?" said Rick. I think he already understood; he just didn't want to face it any more than I did. "You saying we gotta just . . . go? Just, like . . . leave you alone here? Just say good-bye and not see you anymore and just hope you don't get arrested or killed?"

"Pretty much," I told him. "That's pretty much what I'm saying. Yeah."

"Well, I won't," said Rick. "I'm not doing that. It's crazy." No one said anything. "It's crazy," Rick repeated, looking around at the others for support.

Miler took one of his hands out from behind his head. He reached over with it and patted Rick's ankle.

"It's not crazy, Rick-O," he said. "It's true. I guess we all know it."

"No," said Rick. "No, man. We can't just leave him alone here."

"We won't just leave him," said Beth. "We'll bring him supplies. Food and some money and some new clothes and shoes."

"Beth," I said, "I can't take those things."

"Yes, you can," said Beth. "In fact, you have to. You have to let us help you, Charlie. We need to."

"That's true too," said Miler.

Rick nodded heavily. His big round face looked so

sad it almost seemed angry. "See, that's the thing, Charlie. That's the thing you don't get about all this. You being out there—alone—with everyone after you—that's just like— it's just like a piece of us is out there."

"That's right," said Josh.

"That's right," said Miler.

"Every time we see on television that you got chased or attacked or accused of doing something we know you didn't do, that's just like it was happening to us too."

"Even when we don't see it," said Beth. "Even when we don't know it's happening, it's like it's happening to us."

The guys nodded.

"You gotta let us help you," said Rick. "Then it's like we're not all so far away from each other."

"Right," said Josh. "I mean, if we can at least give you some stuff to take with you, then it's like you can look at it and know we're there and we'll know you're doing that and we'll know you're there. It'll be like . . . I don't know . . ." He couldn't find the words.

"Like the old days," said Miler. "At lunch and stuff."

Rick smiled at the memory. "Yeah, like when we'd be all laughing and everything."

They were quiet a second.

Then Rick added, "Man, I miss that."

Then we were all quiet. I felt the cool autumn air from the window on my neck, and a thought flashed through my mind that it wasn't the chill air at all but the chill finger of that cowled woman in the graveyard as she reached out her hand trying to stop the things she loved from dying.

"Hey, I have an idea," said Josh, making his voice bright.

"Uh-oh," said Rick. "We're in trouble now."

"No, really. I could set up webcams for all of us. You know, Charlie, so maybe sometimes you could stop in at one of those cybercafes or something and get a computer and we could see each other."

"Hey," said Rick, surprised. "That's actually a good idea. That's actually not stupid."

"And anyway," said Beth, her voice brighter too, "it's not like it's going to be forever or anything. Charlie's going to find out who killed Alex, and then the police will understand they have the wrong person and they'll help him find . . ." Suddenly her face kind of crumpled up. She put her head down in one hand and sobbed. "I'm sorry. I'm sorry."

Rick and Miler and Josh looked away, looked at the floor, looked anywhere. I went to Beth and tried to put my arms around her, but she waved me off, saying, "I'm okay. I'm sorry, I just . . . I'm okay now."

And she was. I moved away from her.

"Okay," said Josh. He clapped his hands together. "Let's make a plan."

We did. It was a good plan too. First they were going to bring me some stuff I could use: money, food, a backpack, warm clothes, new sneakers. Whatever else they could think of: a good flashlight and one of those sleeping bags that can be crushed down almost to nothing and other stuff like that. Plus, they were going to bring me duplicate car keys and text me to tell me where they'd parked their cars during the day so I could go and get a car if I needed one while I was here. Plus Josh was going to hook them all up with webcams and fix me up with some Internet connections in their names so we could link up with one another sometimes and I could tell them if I needed something, or we could just see one another and talk and they could pass messages on to my parents too. For now, they'd leave me with the laptop so we could still communicate. Later, when I'd left town, I'd be able to get in touch through other computers. If we didn't talk too long or anything, we might do it without being noticed and traced.

"It'll be like you have—what do they call that?" said Rick. "Oh yeah: a support network."

Everyone in the parlor seemed to like that. We all repeated it several times. "A support network, yeah."

Miler said, "It'll be like: The terrorists have guns and bombs and knives and stuff. And the police have cars and sirens and computers and nationwide communication. And you have us."

I tried to laugh. "Sounds like a fair fight to me."

For the rest of the day, Beth and the guys came and went, each of them bringing things they either had at home or had gone out and bought at the store. Josh set up the webcams on each person's computer and we tested them on the laptop. They brought me duplicates of their car keys. They pooled some money for me, and Beth even thought to buy me a wallet to hold it in. Rick brought me an excellent Swiss Army knife with about a dozen tools in it. I promised to leave all the stuff I didn't need in the house when I left so they could come and pick it up.

By the time they were finished with everything, it was almost evening. The sun had fallen low and spread a sort of peaceful, golden light on the stark branches of the trees around the cemetery. I was wearing my fleece, plus a thick windbreaker Beth had lifted from a box her mother had been going to send to the Goodwill. Even so, the air coming in through the broken window had the first touch of night in it and I could feel the cold.

I looked around the room. I had plenty of food to eat now—packaged meat and bread and apples and cheese— a feast practically—all put into lots of plastic containers to keep the mice out. I had cash if I needed to buy anything. I had water and sleeping bags and the computer.

"Place is like the Batcave now," said Rick. "Like the Fortress of Solitude. Charlie Headquarters."

We were all standing around the room, our hands in our pockets, our shoulders hunched against the cold. Our talk had become halting and awkward. We knew it was getting to be time to say good-bye.

Finally, our voices trailed off to nothing.

"Well . . ." said Rick.

"Yeah," said Miler. "Well . . ."

I could feel the sadness settling over us. I imagined it dropping down from the ceiling like a heavy velvet shroud.

"Hey," I said, trying to sound cheerful. "Stay on the Web. I'm gonna turn up on your computer more often than a second-rate starlet."

"Yeah," said Rick. "Only keep your underwear on, all right? I have a weak stomach."

I stepped up to him. We gripped hands, slapped each other's shoulders. I did the same with Miler. The same with Josh.

"You did great today," I told Josh. "You were monster."

"Yeah," he said. "I was monster. Thank you, Charlie."

I watched them file out of the room. I heard their footsteps on the stairs. I heard the front door opening and closing. I knew what they meant about a piece of them being out on the road with me, because I felt like pieces of myself were leaving with them.

Then the house was quiet, and I was there alone in the parlor with Beth.

We talked for a while. We talked about how we would see each other on Josh's webcams. We talked about how Beth would tell me the rest of our story. We talked about how I'd eventually remember everything and how we would get back together and everything would be all right. It was all kind of awkward, though. Kind of halting and strange. I knew we had been in love with each other and I could feel that love coming back to me. But I couldn't remember and she could. She was still further down that road than I was. She had to go slow so that I could catch up.

"I guess in a way I'm lucky," I told her. "I get to fall in love with you twice."

"Charlie . . ." she said, her voice breaking.

"Don't," I said. "Don't, Beth. God has a plan to bring us back together. I'm sure of it."

"I'm sure too. I just hope it's one of his really short-term plans . . ."

Finally, she had to leave.

I stood at the top of the stairs as she walked down them. She was just a shadowy figure in the deeper shadows of the house. Then, when she opened the front door, the golden light of the dying afternoon poured in over her. She paused there and looked back over her shoulder, lifting her face to me where I stood on the landing above her. The gold light glistened on her cheeks where the tears were. My heart ached and I knew even then that she would be part of me forever.

Then the door shut with a thump and she was gone.

I walked back into the empty parlor. I returned to the window. I looked down at the graveyard below. For one more moment, the sunlight held that tinge of gold, making even the cemetery kind of beautiful in some strange, sad way. Then the gold leaked out of the light. The scene became dull and somber. An aura of blue crept into it— the first hint of evening.

I stood there a long time, waiting for night to fall. Waiting until I could go out into the darkness and begin searching for some answers.

PART THREE

CHAPTER TWENTY-THREE

Sensei Mike

There was a time, when I was little, when I first started to learn karate, when Sensei Mike's karate studio seemed to me a very impressive place. More than that: it was almost awe-inspiring. There were ceremonial swords hanging on one wall and a large American flag hanging on another. There were rank belts hung in their order, white to black, above the room-length mirror on the third wall. There was a plaster divider that marked the dojo off from the foyer, and on top of the divider there were these little wooden statues of Chinese monks in cool karate postures or wielding cool weapons like battle-axes and maces. Back when I was a kid, all these things struck me as sort of solemn and important, as if they were images of some great ideal I had to live up to, some mighty tradition I was becoming part of. The place seemed almost like a church to me.

Over time, as I grew older, bigger, I began to see the karate school more the way it really was. It was really just a little storefront place in a local mall. Kind of cramped and ill-equipped and even shabby in a way. But by then, I understood that what was big and important and mysterious about the place didn't come from the building. It came from the ideas and from the teachers—from Sensei Mike especially. It came from what he understood karate to be and what it meant to him. He carried those meanings inside him and, by teaching his students, he planted them inside us. If we had just learned to fight, just learned to punch and kick and so on, then the place would've been as small and shabby as it looked. But what we really learned was how to discipline ourselves, how to keep our minds and bodies under our own control, how to win with grace and lose with courage and keep fighting no matter what.

And we learned how to pay attention—that was maybe the most important thing of all.

So I guess what I'm saying is that the karate school really was as big and impressive and awe-inspiring as I thought it was when I was a little kid, only in a different way, a deeper way that I had to learn to understand. I guess there's a lot of stuff that's like that when you come to think about it.

That night, around nine o'clock, I sat in the Eastfield Mall parking lot and watched the dojo. Through the storefront window, I could see the last students of the day going through their motions.

I was in Rick's car, a sleek, red Civic. He'd left it for me at the Lake Center Mall—the one near the Ghost Mansion—and driven home with Josh. That way I would have something to drive for the rest of the night.

I sat in the car, parked not far from the dojo. I peered out through the windshield at the storefront. There were two kids having a lesson in there, both about my age, both brown belts. Mike had them doing maneuvers on each other—sort of programmed defense techniques that teach certain classic moves you can adapt and use later for real fighting. One student would throw a punch at the other and the other would block it or dodge it and then go through the motions that would bring the attacker down to the floor. Then they'd change sides and the other student would throw the punch while the first one did the defense.

About a million thoughts went through my mind as I watched them. I don't know how many times I'd been in the dojo going through the same motions they were going through now. It was a lot. I wished I was in there with them, using karate as a way to get exercise and learn discipline, instead of having to use it to defend myself. When I was in training at the dojo, I used to have daydreams about getting in fights and beating up bad guys and rescuing girls who were in trouble—you know, the usual daydreams guys have. But now that I'd actually had to fight for real, I wished I was back in the dojo having daydreams. I wished I'd never have to be in a real fight ever again.

And I was thinking about Mike. I was watching him as he sort of skipped around the two brown-belt students, as he followed their moves and talked to them, correcting their techniques, demonstrating how to do it right. I was too far away to hear his voice for real, but I could hear him in my imagination, saying, *"Come on, you chuckleheads, focus, take charge of your own minds."*

Had Paul Hunt been telling Josh the truth? I wondered. Had Alex really been coming to see Sensei Mike the night he was killed? Why? Why would they be meeting in secret like that? Hunt had said that Alex was doing some kind of business with adults, people in town who seemed decent and respectable but were really running some kind of criminal enterprise. Was he lying? Was he just making stuff up to sound important? Or was it possible Mike wasn't who I thought he was? Was it possible the best, smartest, wisest teacher I ever had was not who I thought he was at all?

I guess it came down once again to the question that had been buzzing around in my mind all this time: How can you tell who the bad guys and good guys are? How can you even tell whether you're a bad guy or a good guy? I mean, Mike told me the good guys were the people who were moving toward the light. But how did you know if you were moving in the right direction? So many people say so many different things, believe so many different things. How can you tell whether you're on the right side or not?

I sat in the Civic with all those thoughts running through my mind, kind of racing around and crashing into one another. I guess I kind of drifted off into my own private world. Then, when I came back to myself, I saw through the dojo's storefront that the last lesson of the day was over. The students were giving their quick karate-style bows of respect to the American flag and to Sensei Mike. Then they knelt in the meditation position for a few minutes. Finally, Mike dismissed the class.

I sat and watched while the students helped Mike clean up the dojo for the day. It was getting close to ten o'clock when they finally finished. Mike watched them carrying their equipment bags out the door, giving each a good-night punch on the shoulder as they went past. Then the door swung shut and Mike was alone. I watched as he disappeared into the changing room in back to get out of his gi and put on his street clothes.

I waited in the car a few more minutes. I scanned the parking lot. It was late now. A lot of the mall stores were closed. But there were still plenty of cars parked around. People were still using the supermarket and the restaurants and the Starbucks, all of which stayed open late. That was a good thing from my point of view. As long as there were people in the mall, I could blend in. I doubted anyone would recognize me in the dark. I didn't see any cops patrolling either.

I faced forward in time to see Mike come out of the

back room. He was dressed in jeans now and a gray sweat-shirt that said US Army on the front. He came across the dojo to the foyer and then went into his office off to the side.

I moved quickly. I got out of the car and started walk-ing directly toward the dojo, trying not to look left or right. My heart started beating really hard. I didn't know how Mike would react when he saw me again. I didn't know how he'd react when I asked him about Alex.

I could see Mike inside through the slats of the vene-tian blinds on his office window. He was getting ready to close up shop. He was standing at his desk in the office, bending over his computer, shutting it down. I saw the white light of the monitor on his face for a moment. Then the light went out.

By the time I reached the door, I was so nervous I could hardly breathe. I pushed the door open.

I stepped in quietly, but I guess Mike heard the door swing shut. He called from the office.

"We're closed."

Then he stepped into the office doorway.

He didn't look any different than I remembered. He wasn't like my friends—teenagers who change so much in a year. He still had the black hair, neatly combed, and the big mustache. He still had that permanent sardonic smile and the sad, secret laughter in his eyes—even now—even when he saw me and froze where he was.

It was really good to see him after all this time. I hoped he wouldn't turn me away.

There was no big reaction. Mike just gave a quiet snort, that's all. "Hey, Charlie," he said.

"Hey, Mike. You don't look all that surprised to see me."

He shook his head. "I'm not surprised. The police won't be surprised either. They figured you might come here. Maybe you'd better move away from the window, let me close the blinds."

I stepped deeper into the foyer, to the doorway of the dojo. Mike went to the storefront. He peered out briefly into the parking lot—checking for cops, I guess. Then he pulled a string and brought the venetian blinds down over the glass. He turned the rods and the slats shut, so that no one outside could see us. All the while he went on talking to me:

"The police contacted me this morning. After they lost you at the library in Whitney, they figured you were probably on your way to Spring Hill. They asked me to get in touch with them if I saw you." When he was done with the blinds, he turned around and faced me, standing in front of the door. "You took a big chance coming here, chucklehead."

My heart hammering, I watched his eyes, tried to read his thoughts. It was impossible. There was just the same look as always—a look that said something like: This is a crazy world full of chuckleheads doing crazy things. Which I think is pretty much how Mike figured it.

"You gonna do it, Mike?" I asked him. "You gonna turn me in?"

He paused before he answered. "I might. Depends on what you have to say for yourself. You did the wrong thing, breaking out of prison like that, Charlie. You had a fair trial and you were convicted. If you're innocent, you gotta prove it, that's the law. Now you're a fugitive. You're alone. You could get shot by the cops—by anyone who recognizes you and has a gun. Best-case scenario: you get arrested again and thrown back into prison, only now you got penalty time and everyone's more convinced than ever that you're guilty. It was a pretty dumb play, Charlie. Not the way I taught you to think at all."

"Do you think I'm guilty, Mike?"

He gave another snort. "No." He said it just like that, like he had no doubt.

"How do you know? There was a lot of evidence against me."

"There was," he said. "I figure you must've been framed. It must've been something like that. You're no murderer, that's for sure."

"But how do you know?"

"I just know."

"But how, Mike?"

He snorted again and I saw his smile flash beneath the black mustache. He shook his head. "What're you, some kind of doofus? What kind of question is that? We're not talking about whether you're a Republican or a Democrat. We're not even talking about whether you're right or wrong. We're talking about whether you're good or evil. You think people don't know the difference between good and evil? Even evil people know the difference, Charlie, deep down, where they hide it from themselves. We're made that way at the factory, pal. It's how we find our way back." He cocked his head and eyed me sharply. "Is that why you came here? To ask me that? What's this all about?"

It was hard to answer him, hard to talk at all. Things always seemed so clear when Mike was explaining them. It made me wish I had him around to explain them to me all the time.

"I don't remember," I finally managed to tell him.

He narrowed his eyes. "What? You don't remember what?"

"Any of it. The murder. Breaking out of prison. I don't remember anything after the last time I saw Alex. A whole year of my life has gone down some sort of black hole in my mind."

For the first time, Mike looked genuinely surprised. More than that: he looked shocked.

"It's, like, I went to bed one night, the night Alex got murdered, and the next morning I woke up captured by a bunch of terrorists. And now they say I was one of them and they're trying to kill me. And the police are trying to arrest me and . . . I just don't know anything anymore, Sensei."

For a long time, Mike just stood there, not saying anything. Then he let out a breath—a long, whistling breath. He turned away. He put his hands on his hips and looked down at the foyer floor, thinking. It was several seconds before he looked at me again.

"Why did you come here tonight?" he asked me then. "It wasn't just for a philosophical chat about good and evil."

I shook my head. "I heard something. I heard that

Alex was coming to see you. The night he was murdered—I heard you guys had some kind of secret meeting arranged."

It was the second time I'd surprised him. His eyebrows shot up. "Really? It must've been a pretty big secret. Even I didn't know about it."

"Well, that's what I heard."

"From where?"

"A friend of Alex's named Paul Hunt."

"Good guy?"

"No. But I think he was telling the truth."

Mike went on looking my way, but I could tell he was staring past me, through me, thinking, thinking. Then, slowly, his lips curled and his teeth showed under his mustache as he broke into a smile. His focus shifted and now he was looking at me for real. "Ah, okay. I get it now. You don't remember anything so you don't remember whether you killed Alex or not."

I nodded.

"So what're you trying to do—you trying to solve Alex's murder yourself?"

"Yeah."

"And you asked around and you found out he was coming to see me."

"That's right."

"I get it. You're so messed up in your head, you don't even know whether you're a good guy or not. So how can you know what I am?"

I felt my face get hot. Suddenly I felt ashamed—ashamed for suspecting Mike could be some kind of secret criminal. "Sure I know," I mumbled to him.

"Sure you do. You just forgot, that's all."

I put my hand on my forehead and massaged it, as if I had a headache. Really, I just couldn't stand to look Mike in the eyes. In a lot of ways I knew Mike better than I knew anyone. I knew Mike was a good guy. I knew it deep down, all the way down. I knew he wasn't any kind of criminal or terrorist or anything. I wondered if maybe—maybe if I could just clear my head for a little while—maybe I would know that about myself too.

"I didn't know Alex was coming to see me," Mike said then. "But if he was, I'm pretty sure I know why."

"Never mind," I said, still averting my eyes, still ashamed of doubting him. "You don't have to tell me."

"I know I don't. But I will." He moved around me until he was standing in front of the door. He folded his arms across his chest so that it looked like he meant to block my way out, keep me from escaping. He gazed at me and waited—waited until my gaze met his. Then he said, "About two or three weeks before he died, I bumped into Alex at the library. I recognized him because he used to come in with you to take karate lessons—remember that? You were both pretty small back then, but I recognized him all the same. And I remembered you'd mentioned at some point that he was having problems. He didn't look good, that's for sure. He looked—I don't know what the word is. Hunched-up and secretive. Like he was hiding something. Furtive—that's it. Anyway, I went over to say hello, you know, maybe talk to him, see if there was something I could do to help out. He was working on one of the library computers. When he noticed me coming up behind him, he shut it down really fast, like he didn't want me to see what he was looking at. But those library computers, you know, they're kind of slow and I got a look at the page. It had some kind of title like Real True America or something. I tried to find it once, but I couldn't, so that might not be the exact name. Anyway, I talked to him. He told me about what was going on at his house, all the trouble he was having. He seemed pretty upset, pretty confused. I told him he ought to drop by to see me, talk things out. He said he might—he might just do that—and he sounded like he would too. So I guess maybe that's why he was in the mall, that's what he was planning to do."

"You mean, you think he just needed someone to talk to?" I said. "But why would he want to keep that secret?"

"I don't know. It's a good question. Maybe someone didn't want him to talk to me. Or maybe he was just embarrassed that he needed help. A lot of guys are."

"Did you tell the cops about this?"

"I told them what I knew. I didn't know he was planning to come here that night so it didn't really seem all that important."

I nodded. It made sense. It made a lot more sense than the idea that Mike was some kind of secret criminal, that's for sure. I thought back to the night of the murder. When Alex and I had our big argument, he said all kinds of crazy stuff—about how everything he had learned to believe in—his parents, God, his country—was all false. I could see at the time that he was saying stuff he didn't really think was true. I could see in his eyes that it bothered him. It made sense that he had been on his way to Mike, that he was hoping Mike could set him straight.

"Does that answer your questions?" Mike asked me.

"Yeah," I said sheepishly. "Look, Mike, I didn't mean to say I thought you were involved in anything bad or anything."

"I know what you meant to say."

"It's just all this stuff—and not being able to remember—it's confusing."

"I know it is. And that's why . . ." He reached up and stroked his mustache as if he was thinking. Then he said, "That's why I'm going to have to turn you in."

For a second, I didn't really hear him, didn't really understand what he'd said. Then I did. My mouth opened, but I couldn't answer. I felt sick inside. I felt like my heart was speeding up and falling down at the same time. "Turn me in?"

Mike nodded slowly, sadly.

"Mike . . ." I said. "You can't. The police . . . they'll arrest me."

"Yeah," said Mike with a kind of laugh that wasn't a laugh. "I actually figured that out myself. I'm sorry, pal. I have to do it."

"But why?"

"Because look at you, man. I can't let you leave here and go wandering off. You're in a lot of trouble and a lot of danger and you're not thinking straight. You can't remember anything. You're all confused about what's what. Plus, it sounds like you've gotten yourself involved with some pretty-bad-news hombres. If you don't get off the streets, they could do you some real damage."

"I know, Mike, but . . . I can handle it."

"Maybe. But for how long? And for what? So you can live on the run. So you can live as a criminal. Look, I know being in prison is no picnic. But we'll get you out. You're innocent. We all know it and we're gonna prove it. Out here, you're just going to get yourself killed. Think of your mom, Charlie. Your mom and dad, they're practically dying with worry about you. They're terrified every day, every minute, just waiting to hear you've been shot by some cop somewhere."

"But Mike, listen . . ."

"It's for your own good, Charlie, your own protection. You're in over your head. I've got to hand you over."

I took a step toward him, toward the door. He held out his hand like a policeman stopping traffic. Our eyes met. I could see just by looking at him that he didn't want to do this. But I could also see that he would do it because he thought it was right.

"Look . . ." I said. "You've got to let me go. I've got to prove I didn't kill Alex."

"Charlie, you don't know what you sound like. You're outnumbered, you're outgunned. You can't remember anything. What can you do that we can't do for you? I mean, you escaped so soon after the trial, your folks didn't even have time to file an appeal. You gotta give the system a chance to work, man. It's the best way. Better than this."

"Mike, I just need some time . . ."

He hesitated. I don't think I'd ever seen Mike look so indecisive before. He wasn't sure he was doing the right thing, but he felt he had no choice. If I could just convince him . . .

"Sorry, chucklehead," he said now. "Don't make this harder on me than it already is."

He stepped away from the door. He started walking toward his office, toward his phone.

I seized the moment. I leapt for the door.

But Mike was too fast. The next moment, he had me. He grabbed me by my belt and the back of my collar. He hurled me backward so that I went stumbling across the foyer, through the doorway into the dojo. I tripped on the threshold and went down, my butt hitting the carpeted floor with a thud.

Mike, meanwhile, went back to his office door. But he

didn't go in. There was a plastic box on the wall there. It had a little flap. He pulled it open. I could see what it was: the alarm system.

Mike pressed a button. A bell began ringing, not in the dojo but out in the mall where any passing cop could hear it.

"The police won't show up right away," he told me. "The alarm company will call here first. Then, when I don't answer, they'll call the cops. It usually takes about five, ten minutes before they get here."

I scrambled to my feet just inside the dojo. "Please, Mike, don't do it; let me go."

"No can do, my friend. This is for the best."

He was still standing by the office door, by the alarm box. There was still a path open between him and the door. I knew there was no rear exit. I didn't see what else I could do.

I rushed for the door again.

Mike grabbed me by the arm. I swung my arm around, breaking his grip—just as he taught me to do.

But as I swung my arm, he struck me in the nerve center in the armpit—not hard, but hard enough to stun me with the pain. I cried out. Mike got in front of me. He lifted his foot and planted a kick in my midsection—it was more of a push than a kick—not trying to hurt me, just trying to knock me back.

Which it did. Once again, I stumbled back into the dojo.

This time, Mike followed me in, blocking my way.

"What're you gonna do, Charlie. Fight me?" he asked.

I staggered until I could regain my balance. Then I faced him. I saw the glint of humor in his eyes—humor and sadness both.

I couldn't believe what I was saying—even though I knew I had to say it.

"Yeah. Yeah, I'm gonna fight you, Mike. I'm not going back to prison without a fight."

Mike shrugged. "It's a fight you can't win," he told me.

But he didn't have to tell me that. I already knew.

CHAPTER TWENTY-FOUR

A Fight I Couldn't Win

Mike took another step into the dojo. I took another step back away from him. I had to find a way past him—and quick—before the alarm company called the police, before the police arrived. Five minutes. Ten at most.

But how? Whatever fighting tricks I knew, Mike had taught me. However long and hard I'd practiced, he'd practiced more. Plus, he'd been in the army, in real battles in Iraq and Afghanistan. How could I neutralize him even long enough to get to the door?

The ringing of the alarm went on outside, a steady bell.

And I thought: *the phone*. The alarm company was about to call to make sure the alarm hadn't gone off by accident. That meant the phone in the office was about to ring. Maybe that would draw Mike's attention, distract him just for a second. If I could use that second to knock him out of the way . . .

Then the phone rang—and I struck.

It was the strangest feeling. To attack my own teacher. To attack the guy who'd been such a help and a guide to me all the time I was growing up. It wasn't just karate either. Sometimes there had been things I wanted to talk about that I somehow couldn't say to my mom or dad. I could always say them to Mike. Sometimes there were things Mom and Dad just didn't understand. Mike always did. He was what I guess you'd call a mentor. He was the last person in the world I wanted to attack.

But I had to do it. I had to get past him. I had to prove I didn't kill Alex—even if I could only prove it to myself.

So when the phone rang—when Mike's eyes shifted toward it reflexively—just a little, just for a second—I was ready. I shot a swift high kick straight for Mike's chest, hoping to knock him back and out of the way.

I actually managed to take him by surprise. I don't think he really believed I'd try it. He didn't have time to dodge—the best defense against a kick. But he was so good, it didn't matter. He curled himself up, pulling his chest away from the kick so that my foot struck without any real power. Then he crossed his arms, trapping my foot between them.

I knew that move—Mike had taught it to me. I knew he would twist my leg next and throw me over to the side.

But Mike had taught me the defense against that, too, so I used it. I hopped in close on one leg and tried to hit him in the mouth with the heel of my palm.

Of course, he knew I was going to do that. He turned aside and tossed me away so that my blow flew right past him—and so did I.

And now he was to the side of me and came in on the attack. He tried to wrap his arm around my throat in a choke hold. He'd be able to knock me out in about three seconds like that.

I couldn't let it happen. Quickly, I slipped underneath his arm just the way he'd always shown me. Then I tried to push him to the side so I could make an escape route to the door.

Before I could, he snapped his elbow back into my

chest and then snapped a backhanded fist into my face. He could've broken my nose with that, but he hit me in the cheek instead because he was trying not to hurt me too badly. It stung plenty, though—and he followed it up with a left-handed blow to the belly that knocked the wind out of me.

All the same, I tried to fight back, tried to throw a right over his punch into the side of his head.

Mike ducked the punch so fast it was as if he'd disappeared from in front of me. Another punch hit me in the belly—a right this time, much harder. I gasped out air and nearly doubled over. Then Mike was behind me.

He chopped me in the back of the neck. He could've killed me with a blow like that, but his control was pinpoint perfect. He hit me just hard enough to send a burst of pain shooting through my head and white sparks exploded in front of my eyes.

My knees buckled and I went down. I had just enough sense left to drop to my shoulder and roll. I leapt to my feet again, throwing my hands on guard just the way Mike had taught me. But to be honest, I was dazed. If Mike had come after me then, he probably could've finished me off pretty easily.

But he didn't attack. He just stood where he was in

the middle of the dojo. He shook his head and stroked his mustache in that way he did when he wanted to hide a smile.

"That was pretty good, chucklehead," he said. "I guess I taught you well. You almost had me for . . ."

I broke for the door. Mike should've known better than to start talking. It's always the best time to make a move—he taught me that.

I was out of the dojo and through the foyer. I was at the door, reaching for it, grabbing it—when Mike caught up to me.

But I was waiting for that, ready for it. The second I felt his hand on my collar, I changed direction as suddenly as I could. I braked on the balls of my feet and spun around. I knocked his hand off me with my left forearm. I shot my open hand at his chest, just trying to push him back. I could've aimed for his throat, but I didn't want to hurt him any more than he wanted to hurt me.

I shouldn't have worried about it. The blow never landed anyway. Mike knocked it away with a left cross-body block and whacked me on the side of the head with his right. It was another blow that could've been a lot worse, but Mike kept his hand open so it was more of a slap than anything else. Still, it rattled me, stunned me—and the next moment Mike had my arm twisted behind me and forced me away from the door, back into the dojo.

He let me go, giving me an extra shove so I went stumbling a few steps away from him. I turned around, breathing hard. Mike just stood there, blocking the way out of the dojo, waiting to see if I would try to get past him again.

I didn't. What was the point? I knew I couldn't beat him. He knew every move I knew and some I didn't. And he knew them all a lot better than I did, maybe better than I ever would.

He stroked his mustache again. "I'll tell you something, Charlie," he said. "You're the best student I ever had." I was glad to see he was breathing kind of hard himself, though nowhere near as hard as I was. "In fact, you're one of the best fighters I've ever seen and I've seen some good ones. Another five years, a little more real-life, maybe some military training, you might even be able to take me. But not today."

I nodded. I knew he was right. I bent forward, resting my hands on my thighs, trying to catch my breath, trying to shake off the pain in my gut and the daze in my head.

The phone had stopped ringing now. I noticed the alarm bell had stopped ringing too. The alarm company must've turned it off on their end. They were probably calling the police now. Another two or three minutes and I'd hear the sirens again, see the flashing lights again. I'd have no way to escape this time.

I had only one chance left. If I couldn't find the right strike to knock Mike out of the way, then I had to find the right words, the right argument, that would make him see why he had to let me go. I had to convince him. And I had to do it now.

"Mike," I said, thinking even as I spoke, searching desperately for the words and the reasoning. "Listen, okay? Just listen to me."

"I'm listening. You have until the police get here."

"You said you figured I was framed, right?"

He nodded. "That's right. You must've been. There was so much evidence against you, there were only two possibilities. Either you were framed or you were guilty. And I know you weren't guilty."

To be honest, I didn't know whether he was right or not, whether I was framed or guilty or whether there was some other explanation altogether. But I did remember what Beth had told me. How she'd described the day I was arrested and what the evidence against me was and so on.

"Some of the traces of blood they found were on my

clothes, remember?" I said. "The clothes I was wearing the last time I saw Alex."

"Yeah, I remember. So?"

"So I gave those clothes to the police myself. I had them at home and I turned them over as soon as they asked for them. No one touched them except for me and the police."

Mike made an impatient gesture with his hand. "So what?"

"Well, how'd the evidence get on my clothes, Mike? How'd the blood get on them?"

"So what're you saying? That you're guilty?"

"Maybe. Like you said: guilty or framed. And if I was framed, then it must've been the police who framed me."

Mike's eyes went wide. "What? Oh, come on!"

"No, listen. Listen. They were the only people who had the clothes, right? Them and me. Who else could've put Alex's blood on them?"

He gave a wave of his hand, made a dismissive noise. "Nice try, Charlie, but that's nuts. That doesn't make any sense at all. I know a lot of the cops in this town. They're straight-arrow, every one of them."

"You can't know them all."

"No. But enough. It's a good department."

"Then I must be guilty," I said. "You said it yourself. Either I was framed or I'm guilty. If I was framed, it had to be someone on the police force who did it. Or at least it had to be someone who could get to the evidence while it was in police custody. Maybe it was the prosecutor or someone in his office. I don't know. But it had to be someone like that. Someone in authority."

For a moment Mike didn't answer, and a little flutter of hope went through me. I could see the logic of it working on him. It was working on me too. I hadn't really thought it through before, but now that I'd said it, it did make a certain amount of sense, didn't it? If I wasn't guilty, then where did the evidence come from? Blood on my clothing. Fingerprints and DNA on the knife. If I wasn't guilty, how could it all get there?

"I never even owned a combat knife, Mike," I said, thinking out loud. "How could it have my fingerprints on it and my DNA? If I was framed, it had to be by someone in power, someone who could get at the evidence and at me."

When I stopped speaking, we were both silent again. And in the silence, I heard them: the sirens. Off at a distance somewhere, but coming fast. Mike heard them too. We both glanced in the direction of the door.

"Mike, listen," I said. "Either I'm guilty or you may be giving me over to the very people who set me up in the first place."

"I'm telling you," Mike said, "the police wouldn't do that. I know them . . ."

But he didn't sound as sure as he did before. I kept pressing.

"You don't know all of them. It would only take one. Or the prosecutor. Or someone like that. And that means I'm dangerous to someone, someone in authority, someone who knows the truth. If you let them put me back in prison, you may be putting me just where they want me, just where they can get at me."

"You don't know that," Mike said—but again, he didn't sound so sure.

"You said I broke out of prison before my lawyers could even appeal," I pressed on. "I don't remember, but maybe I did it because I had to. Maybe I knew that if I stayed in prison, I wouldn't live long enough for an appeal."

He looked at me and I looked back. We were both thinking it through. We were both realizing it made sense.

And all the while, the sirens were growing louder. That sound like baying dogs getting close to their prey. It made me sick inside. The police would be here any minute now.

"Mike, please," I said. "Just think about it. If you let me go, at least you know I'll be free to defend myself. If you send me back to prison, you might make me a sitting duck; you may be putting me right where they want me." Mike actually nodded slightly. I couldn't fight him, but my words were getting through. "If you think I'm guilty, turn me over," I said. "But if you think I was framed, you gotta let me go. You gotta let me try to prove it. Someone— someone on the inside—is my enemy. If you think I'm innocent, you've got to let me go."

Mike just went on standing there, went on looking at me. Another second went by and then another. The sirens were much louder now. I thought the cops must be almost at the mall. There was no more time . . .

"You're innocent," said Mike then—now he was the one who was thinking out loud. "There's no question you're innocent, not to me. Some things you know because you can prove them. But another man's heart—that's something you have to take on faith. I have faith in you, Charlie. I know you're no killer. And if you really think you have to keep running in order to stay alive"—he turned aside, leaving a path to the door—"then go."

There was no time to say all the things I wanted to say to him, to give him all the thanks he deserved, not just for this, but for everything, all through the years. There was no time to say any of it. Choked up, I gripped his shoulder once as I went past him.

Then I was out of the dojo. Through the foyer. At the door.

"Godspeed, chucklehead," I heard Mike say behind me.

I braced myself and stepped out into the night.

The sirens came closer and closer. At last, I saw the flashing lights of the police cruisers converging on the mall. I saw two cars come screeching to a halt in the parking lot in front of the dojo. I saw a uniformed officer step from each of the cars and I saw the two of them go running to the dojo door.

I saw it all in the rearview mirror of Rick's red Civic. Because by then, I was driving away.

CHAPTER TWENTY-FIVE

Real True America

Back at the Ghost Mansion, I tried to sleep. Maybe I did sleep a little. I don't know. Mostly I lay awake, staring into the dark, wrapped in my sleeping bag against the cold that came in at the windows.

It wasn't the spooky creaking of the old house that disturbed me. It wasn't the scrabbling of the mice in the walls. It wasn't the moaning of the autumn wind in the trees outside or the leaves rattling through the graveyard there or even the thought of the mourning woman, cowled and staring blank-eyed into nothingness.

The ghosts of the haunted house didn't scare me any-more. It was reality that was terrifying. It was my own racing thoughts that wouldn't let me rest.

I kept going back over what I'd said to Mike. I kept thinking about what Beth had told me, about the day I was arrested. I had come to her that morning on the path by the river, she said. I had told her about all the evidence there was against me.

"How could that happen?" she'd asked me.

It was a good question. How could it have happened? How could Alex's blood have been on my clothes? How could my fingerprints have been on the knife that killed him?

And what about Alex? What had he been involved in? Who had he known? Why had he been going to see Mike and why did he want his friends to keep it secret? Who could have killed him if I hadn't?

It was still dark outside when I got up, but I could hear a few birds twittering and I knew that dawn was near.

I crawled out of the sleeping bag. I stood bouncing on my toes and hugging myself, shivering in the cold. When I warmed up a little, I sat cross-legged in front of the laptop Josh had left for me. I turned it on.

I had to use the computer sparingly. Josh had given

me two batteries, but with no electricity in the house there was no easy way to recharge them. I figured I'd get about four hours of use from them all told.

I went to work. I called up a search engine and started looking for the site called something like Real True America—the site Mike had seen Alex looking at when he was at the library.

It wasn't easy to find. It took me nearly forty-five minutes of trying different combinations. It turned out what I was looking for was not a site, but a page on a site that had a harmless-looking title like "A Student's Guide to American History."

The page was headlined: "Real True America: Debunking the Myths, Getting the Facts Straight." There were a lot of links on the page, but I only had to go to a few of them before I realized what they were. Basically it was a list of every bad thing that had ever happened in this country, everything people had ever done wrong. You know the stuff: slavery and some of the unfair attacks on American Indians and so on. Some of it really was bad and some of it only looked bad when taken out of its historical context. And there was none of the good stuff at all. Nothing about the Constitution and the way it preserved and protected the freedom God gave people to do and think and become whatever they could. Nothing about the fact that America's influence had brought that freedom to places where it had never been and protected it in places where it was under attack. There's so much about this country that is unique in history and great for humankind. But none of that was there. It was only about the bad stuff people do, which happens in America just like it happens everywhere else.

It's easy to make something sound bad if you only tell one side of the story. That's what they did here.

So this was the sort of stuff Alex was looking at. I scrolled through it quickly, keeping track of my battery meter as it got lower and lower. I was about to turn the computer off, when I found a link that said, "The Great Proposition." It sounded important, so I hit it and was taken to another page.

This is what it said:

For too long, America has sought to impose its way of life on the rest of the world. It's got to stop. Americans have got to learn that the so-called "Truths" they hold "self-evident" aren't really truths at all, but just cultural perspectives, which might be different somewhere else. Concepts like "liberty"—which can lead to unfairness—or freedom of speech—which allows people to say offensive things—or "rights" given us by a "Creator" to such selfish goals as "the pursuit of happiness"— these may seem good to you, but who's to say they are good for everyone? To believe in any absolute truth is oppressive. *Absolutism is the meat of tyrants. Real morality is always relative to situations and cultural traditions.*

I caught my breath as the last words seemed to leap out at me from the monitor. I remembered those words. I remembered when Mr. Sherman had spoken them to me in class, almost exactly as they were written there on the page. Had he read it here?

Or had he written it?

The moment the thought occurred to me, it made a kind of sense. I didn't know whether Mr. Sherman and Alex had ever talked to each other, but if they had, I could really see Sherman filling Alex's head with a lot of the ideas that seemed to confuse him just before the end. That didn't mean Sherman was some kind of villain or something. He was entitled to his opinions just like anyone.

But it might mean that he knew a lot more about how Alex had gotten killed than he let on.

I remembered something else too. I remembered how Beth had told me that Mr. Sherman was my friend during my trial, that he stuck with me and believed in me and talked to me all the time. That hadn't made a lot of sense to me when she said it, but what if he'd been trying to sell me the same ideas he'd sold to Alex?

As I sat there, staring at the words, trying to figure out what it all meant, a noise came out of the computer's speaker. It was kind of like the sound of a door opening—a signal that one of my friends had come online. In one corner of my computer, there was a list of my friends: Beth, Josh, Rick, and Miler. It was Beth who had just signed on.

I clicked on the webcam symbol and waited to see if she would turn on the camera Josh had given her. A moment later, there she was, her face filling the monitor. She was wearing a bathrobe and her hair was in tangles, but she was pretty anyway, and her eyes were smiling and sweet. Suddenly the Ghost Mansion didn't seem so bleak and empty.

I saw her look over her shoulder as if she was worried her parents would come in and see me on the screen. She leaned into the machine and spoke in a low voice as if she didn't want anyone to hear.

"Hi," she said.

"Hi."

"I hoped you'd be there. Are you all right? Did you get any sleep? Did you have enough to eat?"

"Yeah, yeah, I'm fine, I'm fine. Don't worry so much."

She gave a wry little laugh. "You can't have that wish, Charlie. I worry a lot."

I smiled. It was actually kind of nice to have her worry about me. "I was just looking at some stuff, trying to figure some things out."

"How's it going? You find anything?"

"I'm not sure. You remember you said Mr. Sherman was my friend during the trial."

"Uh-huh. He was great. He talked to you almost every day. You know, trying to keep your spirits up and everything."

"You ever hear any of our conversations?"

I could see her thinking about it. She shrugged. "Not really. Nothing important anyway. But I remember you guys had lunch a bunch of times during the trial and took a couple of drives together, just the two of you."

I nodded. I wondered. Was Sherman using our talks

275

to try to convince me of the stuff I'd just seen on the Web site? To try to turn me against my country and the things I knew were true? Was he the one who'd been trying to convince Alex?

Beth's voice came through the computer, tinny-sounding on the little speaker, but still warm and nice, like her. "What are you thinking?"

"I'm just thinking: a guy who's on trial—who maybe thinks he's being framed by the government or by the police—he might be pretty bitter, you know. He might be open to someone telling him bad stuff about his country."

"I guess. So?"

Before I could answer her, there was another noise like a door opening. Josh had signed on. I would've preferred to go on talking to Beth alone, but I needed to talk to Josh too. I clicked the webcam symbol again. A second later, the screen space divided and there was Josh's geeky, pasty face next to Beth, blinking out at me through his glasses.

"Hello, you young lovers, you," he said with a big, stupid grin that became even bigger and stupider as he leaned into his webcam. "Just the sight of your fresh faces makes these old bones come alive again."

I shook my head. "Listen, you idiot. I need you to help me out with something."

"I live to serve."

"What if I needed to get into somebody else's computer? Find out what kind of stuff he had on there."

He thought about it. "Would this someone's computer be password-protected?"

"Probably, yeah. Almost definitely."

"I might be able to set you up with an e-mail that would break into his computer, but it would depend on him opening the mail and it might take some time. Also, his protection software might spot it."

"No," I said. "That's no good. I need to do this fast."

"Okay," said Josh—and now he sounded like he was really enjoying himself. "I'm gonna send you something really cool, some really cool software. It's called Private Eye. All you gotta do is download it onto a disk, personalize it to your computer, then upload onto the other guy's computer. Then, on your computer, you'll be able to read every keystroke he makes, his e-mails, everything. And when he types in his password, you'll get it—and then you can get into his computer and get anything you want."

"Cool," I said.

"Wait a minute," said Beth. "How's he going to do

that? How's he going to upload the program onto the person's computer?"

Josh rolled his eyes. "Well, duh, Beth. He goes to the guy's computer and puts the disk in."

"Well . . . that's not legal, is it?"

Josh smacked himself in the face with both hands as if this was the stupidest thing he'd ever heard.

"Beth," I said gently. "I'm already wanted for murder. It's not gonna matter much if they tack on a charge of breaking into a guy's computer. They can't exactly send me away for longer than life."

"I know," she said. "But . . . if you have to go to the person's computer yourself, you could be caught."

"He could be caught anyway!" Josh cried out. He laughed at her, a wild high laugh. He was being incredibly obnoxious.

"Josh," I said.

He laughed wildly some more. "What, dude?"

"Shut up."

"Oh." He stopped laughing. "Look, you could send it to him in an e-mail, but it's more dangerous that way and he might not execute the file."

"Just send me the program. I'll take care of it."

"Right, right. Here it comes."

I saw Josh fidgeting around on the monitor. A moment passed, then a file came over. I opened it and a download bar appeared at the bottom of my screen and started filling up quickly.

"Also, I need some way to keep my computer charged a little longer," I said.

"No problem. You get my car today. I'll leave it at Lake Center with a wire under the front seat. You can hook up to the lighter slot. Oh, and one other thing."

"What's that?"

"Don't let anyone find out you put this program in or they'll be able to trace it right to you. It's just like you're visiting a Web site. It's really easy for them to find your physical location. Seriously. If they have the right software, it'd take them about a second."

"Charlie," said Beth, "this sounds really dangerous. Please be careful."

"Beeee caaaaareful, Charrrlie," Josh sang in a falsetto voice, imitating Beth.

Another door-sound came over the computer. Then Rick was onscreen.

"What's going on?" he said.

"Josh is making fun of Beth because she cares what happens to me," I said.

"Nice, Josh," said Rick. "What are you, ten years old?"

There was another door sound. Miler. Now the screen was divided into four segments. All my friends were online.

"What's happening?" said Miler.

"Josh is ten," said Rick.

"Hey, Josh, happy birthday."

"Very funny."

"Will anyone see Mr. Sherman today?" I asked.

"I will," said Rick. "My stats class is in the room right next to his."

"What time?"

"Eleven a.m."

"Perfect. Do me a favor," I said. "Text me when you have him in sight."

"I will do it, *mein kommandant.*"

The download bar was filled. "Program complete," the message said.

"All right, that's it," I said. "I gotta jump off to save my batteries."

"Beeeee caaaaareful, Chaaaarrrrliie," Josh sang falsetto again.

I moved the cursor and turned off his webcam. He

winked out into nothingness—which actually improved his personality.

"Take it easy, guys," I said to Rick and Miler. Then I turned them off too.

Now it was just Beth again, like it was before.

"I really do have to save my battery," I said.

"Charlie," she said. "I don't care what Josh says. Really do be careful."

I smiled. "No one cares what Josh says. Anyway, it sounds a lot nicer when you say it."

She smiled too.

Then I shut down the computer and the darkness of the Ghost Mansion closed around me and I was alone again.

CHAPTER TWENTY-SIX

Something Unexpected

The text came through at 10:55 that morning: *Sherman in sight.*

Rick was in his statistics class and Mr. Sherman was in the classroom next door. That's what I was waiting to hear.

I left the Ghost Mansion by the back way, my laptop in its case, the case strapped over my shoulder. I moved through the graveyard, the leaves rustling under my feet, the sunlight falling in beams through the branches of the trees.

As I passed the statue of the mourning woman, I felt a chill. Up close, there was something too real about her, as if that reaching hand of hers might suddenly move, might suddenly reach out even farther and grab me.

I kept an eye on her as I went past. I watched her over my shoulder as I went on beneath the trees.

I came to an open field, an expanse of brown grass and garbage. I could see the Lake Center Mall on the other side of it, protected by a screen of shrubbery. I moved toward it to find Josh's car.

I hated traveling by day. It made me feel naked, totally exposed to anyone who might recognize me and call the police. But at the same time, it was a rare treat to feel the sun on me, to see the world in the light, to hear the sounds of the world awake. As I came closer to the mall, I caught glimpses of the parking lot through the gaps in the shrubs. I could see the cars pulling in. I could see women—it was mostly women at this hour, mostly moms—getting out to do their shopping at the supermarket or the drugstore. To them, it was just an ordinary day in Spring Hill. To me, it was everything I'd lost, everything I missed so much. Just the sight of those women made me think of my own mom. I wondered if I'd ever see her again.

When I got to the shrubbery screen, I angled my way

through, the branches scratching my arms. There was a low cinderblock wall after that. I climbed over. I was in the farthest corner of the parking lot where the mall Dumpsters were. I could smell the garbage in them, sour and sharp in the morning air.

I moved past the Dumpsters and spotted Josh's car: the black Camry. I walked toward it purposefully, without looking left or right. I didn't want to do anything suspicious, anything that would attract attention. It would be so easy now for someone to spot me.

I felt a lot better once I was inside the car, behind the wheel, hidden from easy view. I reached under the seat and, sure enough, there was the charging wire Josh had promised me. I hooked it up to my laptop and then plugged it into the slot for the car's cigarette lighter. It would keep the battery charged as long as the engine was running.

I started the engine and headed out.

Mr. Sherman lived in a section of town called the Terrace, I guess because it was at the top of a sloping hill. His house was a narrow two-story with a pitched roof above and a porch below. The house was made of yellow clapboards with brown trim around the windows and the door. It sat dark and quiet on the far end of a neat little square of lawn.

I drove a little past the house, then parked. I got out and looked around. The neighborhood was quiet. There was no traffic on the street, no one out walking. I could see a man mowing a lawn a block away. I could hear the stuttering buzz of the mower as he moved back and forth across the grass. And there was a mailman walking toward me along the sidewalk. He turned down a path to make a delivery about five houses down. Other than that, there was no one in sight.

I started up the slate path that ran over the lawn to Sherman's front door. I figured it would look less suspicious if I just walked up to the house directly, just acted as if I belonged there. I left the laptop in the car, but I had my computer disk with Josh's Private Eye program on it in the pocket of my fleece. I had Rick's Swiss Army knife in my hand, held down low against my leg so no one would notice it.

I stepped up on the porch and went to the door. I rang the doorbell and waited for a minute or so. There was no answer. Now I was sure there was no one inside.

I looked left and right and behind me to make sure there was no one watching.

Then I broke into the house.

Maybe I should have gone around the back. Maybe I

should have looked for an open window. Maybe I should have done a lot of things, but I didn't. I was in a hurry to get inside. I could see the lock on the door was nothing fancy, just a cheap bolt. I knew I could get past it easily.

There was a screen door. I pulled it open, braced it open with my shoulder. I tried the doorknob first. In a safe neighborhood like this, sometimes people just leave their doors unlocked. But no, the lock was set; the knob wouldn't turn. I opened the thinnest blade of the Swiss Army knife. I worked the blade into the space between the door and the jamb. I had to really dig to get it in. The wood of the jamb dented and the paint flaked off. I knew someone might notice this, but I was in too much of a hurry to care.

I worked the blade down to the bolt and forced it back. I pushed the door and with a little more cracking of wood and flaking of paint, it opened.

I went in.

I closed the door behind me and locked it again. Then I had to lean against it for a moment. I was breathing fast and my heart was beating hard. I stayed where I was and listened for any noises in the house. There were none. I started moving.

I was in a small foyer. The stairs were right in front of

me. To my left, I could see a hall and the kitchen at the end of it. To my right, there was a living room. Even with the daylight coming through the windows, it was all mostly in shadow. All the lights in the house were off.

I went to the stairs and started up. I figured if Mr. Sherman had a home office it would be on the second floor somewhere.

Sure enough, when I got to the second-floor landing, I turned and saw the room I wanted at the end of the hall. The door was open. I could see right into it, could see the desk with the computer on it and part of a shelf of books.

I went toward it, past a bedroom, past a bathroom, past some sort of exercise room with a stationary bicycle and some free weights and a TV and stuff. Then I was there.

Sherman's office looked pretty much the way you'd expect a teacher's office to look. It was cramped and messy with shelves on every wall and books on every shelf, some of them stuck in on top of other books because there were too many to fit. There was a big wooden desk against one wall. The computer was there. The computer was off, the screen dark.

I went to the window first. The window looked out on

the side of the house, at a big oak tree and a strip of grass. You could see a section of the street and sidewalk too. When you were close to the glass, you could see about half of the house's driveway. I could still hear the lawn mower going down the block, but I couldn't see anyone out there.

I went to Sherman's computer and turned it on.

With a whispered whir, the computer booted—and then stopped. A password screen came on, just the way I'd figured it would. I took the disk with the Private Eye program out of my fleece pocket. I opened the computer's disk drive and slipped the disk in.

The program started playing automatically. It fed directly into the computer's operating system. Some prompts came up. I'd read the instructions earlier and I typed in the proper commands quickly. There was a pause—then the program started to upload into the computer.

A message came onscreen, blinking white letters. It said that 0% of the program had loaded so far—then 1%, 2%, 3% . . . 5% . . . The numbers increased slowly but steadily.

While they climbed, I searched the room.

I went through the desk drawers first. They were all unlocked. I found papers, files—some school stuff, some personal papers, insurance, bank accounts—but nothing that was helpful.

I checked the computer. Ten percent of the Private Eye program had loaded.

I found a filing drawer and looked in there. More papers, more notes. There were files with various names on them. Hotchkiss. Jefferson. Parker. I glanced inside a couple of them, but it just looked like research for some kind of history project.

Fifteen percent of the program had loaded now.

I moved to the bookshelves. I didn't know where to begin looking. I didn't even really know what I was looking for. Something about Alex. Something about me. Anything that would suggest there was some link between Mr. Sherman and that "Real True America" article.

I moved a couple of books aside. Looked behind them. There was nothing. Just a lot of dust.

Then something caught my eye. It was kind of silly, really, nothing important. It was just a book—a book of short stories. But the title of it was *Homeland*. I pulled it off the shelf. The second I did, I knew I had found something. The book didn't feel right. It didn't feel heavy enough. It felt hollow. I opened it.

Sure enough, the pages inside had been cut away to

make a hiding place. In the hiding place, there were photographs.

I lifted them out. They were snapshots. They all showed one man. A tall man, bald, serious-looking. I don't know how old—forty or fifty maybe. He was wearing a black suit and a dark tie. He looked as if he didn't know someone was taking his picture.

In the first few pictures he was just pushing through the door of what looked like a big office building. Then there were more pictures of him walking away. He was on the sidewalk of a busy street, a street in a big city. I could see the tall buildings all around him. In one picture I could even see the street signs on the corner. One sign said Madison Avenue, the other said 54th Street.

There was nothing particularly strange about these photographs, not on the surface anyway. But something about them held me. I had this faint, strange feeling that I knew this man. I went through the pictures again. The first one of him coming through the door, then the second, then the third . . . and on the third, I froze, staring.

There was something reflected on the dark glass of the door. Some letters from a sign in the office building's foyer. A-M-R-E-T-A-W. For a second, the letters meant nothing to me. But then, realizing they were backward in the reflection, I turned them around in my mind: W-A-T-E-R-M-A . . . The last letter was at the very edge of the door. But I was willing to bet there was another letter after it. N—it must've been N. The sign in the foyer said WATERMAN.

I remembered the stranger who had whispered to me just before he freed me from police handcuffs:

You're a better man than you know. Find Waterman.

I stared at the face of the man in the picture. That strange sense that I knew him came back to me. Was this the man I had to find? And if I did find him, would he be an enemy or a friend?

I was still standing there, staring at the photograph, when I heard the front door open downstairs.

I stopped breathing. My whole body went rigid, vibrating like a plucked string.

I heard a soft bang. It was the screen door swinging shut. Then there were footsteps.

I came back to my senses. Quickly, I fumbled the photographs back into the book. I fumbled the book back onto the shelf. I listened, my heart hammering hard.

The footsteps sounded like they were going down the hallway to the kitchen. They sounded like a woman's footsteps because of the way the heels hit the floor—they sounded like a woman's heels. The footsteps went into the kitchen and stopped.

My teeth gritted with care, every muscle tight with fear, I tiptoed across the room, back to the desk. I checked on the computer screen.

The message was now reading 21%, 22%, 23% . . . It seemed to take forever to move from number to number.

The footsteps downstairs started again. They were coming back down the hallway. Coming back toward the front door and the foyer . . . and the stairs.

I stayed very still, my eyes darting back and forth between the office door and the computer. The download reached 25 percent as the footsteps reached the foyer again. They seemed to stop at the bottom of the stairs.

But whoever she was, she didn't come up. Instead I heard the screen door open again and bang shut.

Quickly, I moved back to the window. I looked out, pressing my face to the glass so I could see as much of the street and the driveway as possible.

There was a car in the driveway now. A blue hatchback. The back was open. As I watched, a woman came from the house and moved behind the car. She reached in and when she came out, she was holding a shopping bag. She was bringing groceries into the house.

Sherman's wife. I don't know why, but it had never occurred to me he might be married. He'd never mentioned having a family. I guess I just never thought about it. It's like that with teachers sometimes. You don't think about their private lives. You figure once they leave school for the day, they just sort of disappear until the next day. I guess I figured if Mr. Sherman was at school, then his house would be empty. It was a stupid mistake.

I looked out the window, watching as Mrs. Sherman shut the car's hatchback with her free hand. That must've been the last bag of groceries she was carrying. The car was probably empty now.

She started moving toward the house again.

I stepped back to the desk, back to the computer. The number on the screen was now 32% . . . 33% . . . 34% . . . The Private Eye program kept loading slowly.

I tensed as the screen door banged shut downstairs again. I stood listening helplessly as the footsteps traveled down the hall, as Mrs. Sherman carried her last bag of groceries into the kitchen.

I watched the numbers moving on the computer screen. It was cool in the house, but sweat had begun to gather on my forehead. Now, one drop ran down my temple toward my cheek. I brushed it away quickly.

The Private Eye program was 40 percent downloaded.

I could hear Mrs. Sherman in the kitchen now. I could hear the refrigerator door open. Sure, she'd be putting away the stuff that would spoil first. That's what my mom always did. At least that meant she wouldn't come upstairs right away.

44% . . . 45% . . .

Now I could hear other noises down below in the kitchen. Cabinet doors banging as they opened and closed. Mrs. Sherman was putting the rest of the groceries away, the stuff that wouldn't spoil. What would she do when she was finished? Would she come upstairs?

More sweat was gathering on my forehead and my neck. I couldn't figure out what to do. There was no closet in the room, no place to hide. The only way out was through the window. It wasn't that high. I could probably lower myself down and drop without breaking my leg. But the window was shut. If I opened it, it was sure to make a noise, a rumble. Then Mrs. Sherman would know I was here. On the other hand, if I waited and she came upstairs, I'd have no time to get away.

What then?

I looked at the screen. Fifty percent. Half done. I wiped the beaded sweat off my face and neck with my hand, but

I felt more sweat dampening my armpits, streaming down my sides.

And what if Mrs. Sherman caught me—what about that? I'd just have to get past her somehow and run for it. What else could I do? But then Sherman would know I'd been here, trying to get into his computer. If he suspected I'd downloaded Private Eye, he'd be able to trace me the second I used it, find me at the Ghost Mansion. The program would be useless—and if there was something in Sherman's computer that would help me find out who killed Alex, it would be lost to me.

More noises from the kitchen below. I couldn't figure out what they were at first. Then I could: paper crunching. She was folding up the grocery bags, probably saving them to use for recycling and stuff like my mom did. A few more cabinets opened and closed.

Then the footsteps started again.

Mrs. Sherman came back down the hall, back toward the foyer. My stomach twisted. I was sure she was going to come upstairs this time.

I glanced at the screen: 61% . . . 62% . . . How complicated a program was this? It seemed to be taking forever.

Mrs. Sherman reached the foyer and—just as I

feared—she started up the stairs. I heard her softened footsteps on the carpeted runners as she climbed.

My heart was beating so fast now, my head felt light. But I had to do something. Where I was, at the desk, at the computer, she'd be able simply to turn her head and see me when she reached the second-floor landing. Even if I hid myself from sight, she'd be able to see that the computer was on.

I had to close the door—or at least close it a little. She might notice that. She might remember that it had been open. But it was a chance I had to take.

She was about halfway up the stairs when I started moving. I was at the door in a second. I figured I had to swing the door about two-thirds of the way shut to block her view of the room from the top of the stairs.

I swung the door in as quickly as I could.

It creaked.

The footsteps on the stairs stopped.

There was a moment of silence. I sensed Mrs. Sherman out there on the stairway, listening.

I pressed myself close to a bookshelf, out of sight of the hallway. I stood as still as stone. I felt my breath trapped in my throat as if it were a lead ball. I felt my heart hammering as if it wanted to break free.

"Bill?" Mrs. Sherman called. "Bill, are you home?"

Another moment of silence went by. *Come on*, I thought. *Houses creak all the time. It was nothing. Just the wood settling.* I tried to force the thoughts from my brain into hers.

Maybe it worked. I don't know. But the next moment, Mrs. Sherman started coming up the stairs again.

I heard her footsteps reach the landing. Then they stopped. Was she looking this way? Would she notice that the door had been shut?

I stood where I was, pressed close to the bookshelf, barely breathing, all heartbeat and sweat and waiting.

Another footstep—this one coming toward me.

Then the doorbell rang.

The next moment, Mrs. Sherman's footsteps were headed down the stairs again.

I practically leapt away from the wall, leapt back to the computer.

Eighty-five percent of the program had loaded.

Come on! I thought frantically. *Come on!* I wanted to strangle Josh for giving me such a slow program. It was all my fault for not thinking there might be a Mrs. Sherman, but that didn't matter. I couldn't strangle myself, so I wanted to strangle Josh.

Downstairs, I heard the door open. I heard Mrs. Sherman say, "Oh, hi!" in a friendly voice.

A man answered her, "How you doing? I just need you to sign for this."

It was the mailman. I'd seen him coming toward the house.

"Nice day to work outdoors," Mrs. Sherman said. I could tell she was making conversation while she signed whatever he needed her to sign.

"A lot better than some, that's for sure," the mailman answered.

I watched the numbers on the computer screen climbing: 90% . . . 92% . . . 93% . . .

"There you go. Thanks," I heard Mrs. Sherman say.

"You have a nice day now," said the mailman.

Then the numbers on the screen took a sort of leap—right to 100%. The last bit of the Private Eye program had loaded.

I heard the door shut downstairs. I heard Mrs. Sherman tearing open a package in the foyer.

Moving as fast as I could, I opened the computer's disk drive. Recovered my disk. Slipped it into the pocket of my fleece with one hand and turned off the computer with the other.

I heard Mrs. Sherman's footsteps moving again—but she wasn't coming back up the stairs, she was heading back down the hall, carrying her package toward the kitchen.

I rushed out of the room. Rushed to the top of the stairs. I went down as fast as I could, keeping on the balls of my feet to stay silent, praying the runners wouldn't creak beneath me.

I could hear Mrs. Sherman in the kitchen when I reached the bottom of the stairs. I ducked quickly into the living room. Now she was coming back my way again, headed up the stairs again.

I heard her on the upstairs landing. Heard her moving down the hall toward her husband's office.

And I was moving too. Moving through the rooms until I reached the back door. Moving out into the yard. Moving around the side of the house to the front.

Moving across the lawn to my car, just as fast as I could go.

CHAPTER TWENTY-SEVEN
Private Eye

It was dark when the first signal came. I was back in the upstairs parlor of the Ghost Mansion. I was lying in the sleeping bag, my eyes closed, my thoughts drifting in and out of dreams.

For moments at a time, I would think I was home again, in my own bed, the blankets pulled up around my chin as I waited for my mom to call me and tell me it was time to wake up for school. I had that dream a lot these days. It was always pretty depressing when I woke up and realized it wasn't true, when the reality came back to me—that I was on the run, alone.

I was sinking deeper into sleep, deeper into my dream when the laptop made a noise beside me.

It was a soft two-note musical tone. I knew right away that it was the Private Eye program. It was alerting me that Mr. Sherman had signed on to his home computer.

I sat up quickly. I pulled the laptop to me. It had come out of sleep mode automatically. The monitor had come on and the Private Eye screen had opened. It was a blank blue screen. A moment later, shimmering white letters began appearing there as if they were being typed by an invisible hand. Everything that Mr. Sherman typed on his computer was appearing here on mine. It was kind of a weird feeling to be spying on someone like that. But it was the only way I'd be able to get the password I needed to break into his machine and find out what he knew about Alex and me.

Strikeback.

That was the first word that appeared on the Private Eye screen. It must've been Sherman's password. *Strikeback.*

There was a pause after that. Then more words began appearing, rolling out fast, then faster, white against the blue background.

At first, there was nothing very interesting. Mr. Sherman seemed to sign on to some kind of e-mail or instant-messaging program. Then he wrote a few messages about appointments and homework and conferences.

Have to re-sked for Monday.

Papers are now back in the system, with comments.

Stuff like that. It went on for another ten minutes or so. Ordinary messages a teacher might send to his students or colleagues or friends. The Private Eye program only intercepted Sherman's keystrokes, so I couldn't see any answers that came back, but I didn't figure they were anything more interesting than what I could see.

Which was pretty much what I was expecting. I didn't really think I was going to learn anything important just sitting here, watching Mr. Sherman's keystrokes. I figured if there was any important information on his computer, I would have to break into his house again and get into the computer using his password and find it myself. I didn't really believe he was going to be sending any e-mails or IMs with any deep, dark secret messages in them.

As it turned out, I was wrong.

After about ten minutes, there was a pause. The messages stopped coming. A white cursor blinked on the blue screen. Then . . .

What are we going to do about West?

My lips parted. I sat up straighter. I stared. I couldn't believe it. Was Sherman sending an IM about me?

I guess there was an answer of some kind, which I couldn't see. Then, a moment later, Sherman typed a message back:

If he was ever in Spring Hill, I think he's gone. It's too hot here with the police after him.

I felt the breath go out of me in a long hiss, as if I were a tire losing its air. It was me they were talking about.

My best guess is he's heading out to Chicago. He must have figured out about our operations there.

That was good. They didn't know I was still in town. But what Chicago operations were they talking about? And why did they think I was onto them?

A pause. Another answer I couldn't read, I guess. Then, again from Sherman's computer:

Yes. But we have to be careful. The police effort to find him is substantial and the last thing we need now is to tangle with the law. You saw what happened at the library.

As the words paused again, I stared at the screen eagerly. My mind raced as I tried to comprehend what it all meant.

It meant Sherman was one of them—that was the

first thing. It meant he was one of the Homelanders. Maybe that meant he was the one who killed Alex too. At least he might know who did.

I took a moment to get hold of this idea: my old history teacher involved with terrorists, with murder. Oddly enough, the idea didn't shock me. It didn't even surprise me, to be honest. He never exactly hid the fact that he disliked America or that he thought ordinary moral ideas were all ridiculous. I guess if you followed Mr. Sherman's thoughts to their logical conclusion, this is where they ended up.

Absolutely. Absolutely.

That was the next message on the Private Eye screen. That didn't tell me much. And the pause that followed was even longer than before.

I waited. The bright glow of the computer screen was the only light in the dark house, an island of light in all that darkness.

Finally, more words appeared on the screen:

A series of explosions this time, right. He can't prevent them. Even if he gets to Chi on time.

Another long pause. I stared into the blue light. Without knowing why, I was beginning to feel jumpy, nervous, as if someone were watching me, as if the light of the computer in the dark house had left me exposed.

I started thinking about the words on the screen. Chicago. A series of explosions. Why did they think I knew about that? In fact, why would they be talking about it so openly on a computer? Weren't they afraid someone might hack in and get the information? Weren't they afraid someone might intercept their messages, just as I was doing right . . . ?

A new thought went through me like a jolt of electricity. I sat straight, tense, hardly breathing. I stopped paying attention to the words on the monitor. Instead, I began to listen to the dark house all around me.

Because this didn't make sense, did it? What was happening here—none of it made any sense. If this was Sherman talking to the Homelanders, they wouldn't expose themselves online like this, would they? They were so secretive, so good at keeping themselves in the shadows. This didn't feel right. It didn't feel real. And so maybe . . .

Maybe it wasn't real. Maybe it was all phony. Maybe it was all just some kind of ploy to fool me, to keep me staring at the screen, to keep my attention diverted while . . .

My hand shot out quickly to the laptop and snapped it shut, turned it off. The light went out, the little parlor plunged into darkness, became one with the surrounding blackness of the Ghost Mansion.

They knew!

Suddenly I was certain of it. They knew about the Private Eye program. Of course. Mrs. Sherman must have told her husband that she thought she'd heard someone in the house. Maybe Sherman himself had seen the marks on the front door and guessed that the house had been broken into. His first thought would have been for the safety of his files, his computer . . .

I'd been careless. I'd been foolish. And now Sherman knew I had been in his office. He knew I had put the Private Eye program in his computer. He—he or someone—was sending false, nonsensical messages to keep my attention diverted to the screen while he traced my address, while he tracked me here.

I sat in the darkness, tense, listening. Did they already know where I was? Were they already on their way? Were they already outside, surrounding me? Or inside, already coming up the stairs.

I listened. For a moment or two, the house seemed silent. But the house was never silent, not really. There were always the creaks and groans of the wood settling. There were always the rapid footsteps of the vermin in the walls. There was always the wind outside in the grave-yard, the leaves tumbling, the crickets in the dark.

Slowly—as slowly as I could—I unfolded from my sitting position and rose to my feet. I took a deep breath and let it out silently. Crouching slightly, I turned to face the parlor doorway.

I had to get out of here. I had to get out of here before they came for me. If I was outside, at least I'd be able to see them approach. At least I'd have room to run.

I started moving. Slowly. Step by step. Trying to keep the floor from creaking. I didn't pause to take any-thing with me. All those great supplies my friends had given me—the sleeping bag, the food, the backpack—there was no time to gather them up. I had to leave them all behind. I'd still have my wallet. The money—that would help. Plus the Swiss Army knife that was still in my pocket. But all the rest—I had to leave it. I just had to go.

I moved on tiptoe, hardly breathing. I moved in the direction of the doorway, which I could just make out—a rectangle of deeper darkness in the darkness of the room. As I moved, I listened with every fiber of myself. Listened for the sound of the door downstairs, or the odd creak of a floorboard. Anything that would let me know the

Homelanders were there with me in the dark. There was nothing.

Now I was at the doorway. Now I was stepping out—slowly, slowly into the hall. I had to get to the stairs. I took another step . . .

And I felt the icy-cold circle of a gun barrel pressed against the side of my head.

Mr. Sherman's voice came out of the darkness.

"Too late, Charlie," he said.

CHAPTER TWENTY-EIGHT

Homelanders 101

The bright beam of a flashlight pierced the dark, shot into my eyes, blinding me. I held my hand up, trying to block the light, trying to see him. I could just make out his figure, dimly visible in the outglow of the beam. He'd pulled the gun back from my head and was holding it close to his body so I couldn't get at it. He waggled the barrel toward the doorway.

"Get back in the room," he said. "Move. Now."

I moved, turning away from the light, hoping my eyes

would adjust. Sherman used the flashlight to show the way back into the parlor.

"Sit down on the floor," he ordered. "Sit cross-legged."

I did what he told me to do. I sat on the floor and crossed my legs. I looked up at him over the flashlight, shielding my eyes with my hand. I could see his face now. His bland, youthful, all-too-familiar face. He was smiling.

"I know you're a dangerous guy, Charlie," he said in a kind of friendly tone, the usual tone a teacher might use talking to one of his students. "But by the time you can untangle yourself from that position, I should be able to shoot you in about five different places."

He had a point. With me sitting cross-legged and him standing above me with a gun, it would be pretty difficult for me to unwind and get at him before he opened fire. But that's not what I was thinking about. I was thinking about the fact that he seemed to have come here alone. That was weird. Why would he do that? If he was one of the Homelanders, why wouldn't he bring some kind of fighting force along with him?

Well, whatever the reason, I figured it was good news. It meant I had a chance against him, if I could figure out a way to get in the first strike.

"I wouldn't think about it if I were you," Sherman said,

as if he were reading my mind. "The only reason you're still alive is because I want some information from you, but if you give me any trouble, believe me, I won't hesitate to kill you."

"Like you killed Alex," I said. The words just came out of me—and as soon as they did, I realized they were true.

He gave a little laugh. "You're the one who killed Alex, Charlie. Remember? The jury said so."

I shook my head. "They were wrong. I never would've done it. Alex was my friend. I wouldn't have murdered him. In fact, I wouldn't murder anyone and you know it. That's why you framed me."

And I realized that was true too. And I felt relief, such incredible relief. I mean, it's kind of crazy, I guess. There I was, sitting there helpless, with Sherman holding a gun on me, ready to kill me, wanting to kill me, and the relief just washed over me like a wave. I hadn't killed Alex. I wouldn't kill Alex. I wasn't a murderer. I knew it.

"It had to be someone Alex knew," I said to Sherman now, squinting up at him over the flashlight beam. "It had to be someone who could approach him in the park in the dead of night. Someone he'd stand there and talk to and argue with. It was you, wasn't it?"

I saw Sherman give an indifferent shrug in the

shadows. He didn't bother to deny it anymore. Why should he? It wasn't as if he would let me live to tell the tale. "You know, it really was your fault to some degree," he said. "Partly your fault, anyway. I spent a lot of time recruiting Alex. We'd already brought him into the fold, educated him about our mission. But then he started to get cold feet, have doubts. That night, I was watching him to see if he was going to give us away to anyone."

I nodded. I knew that was exactly what Alex was going to do that night. He was going to go to Sensei Mike. Mike would've straightened him out, gotten the truth out of him, gotten him to confess that Sherman was recruiting him for the Homelanders. But he never made it to Mike. He got in the car with me instead.

"I followed both of you that night," Sherman said. "I heard you arguing in the car. I don't know what you said exactly, but you really must've reached him, Charlie. By the time I caught up with Alex in the park, he was talking about leaving us, about going to the police. It was too late to let that happen. He knew too much." He shook his head. "A lot of good work wasted. Just like with you."

When he mentioned me, he moved the flashlight so it shone directly into my eyes. I had to turn my head and look away into the darkness.

"With me?" I said.

"You've made things very hard for me in the organization, Charlie. After Alex—and now you—I'm beginning to lose support. In fact, if I don't redeem myself, I could be in quite a bit of hot water. That's why I came here alone tonight. I need to know what happened exactly. Where did I go wrong with you?"

"What do you mean?"

"Well, you seemed . . . You seemed so committed to us. So committed to the cause. I mean, I was counting on that. That's what I told them. I told them, a guy like you, a real true believer, with all your religion, all your blind patriotism, you were a natural for us. I knew if I could just turn all the passion of that belief to our side, you'd become one of the greatest warriors we had."

"But that . . ." *That's stupid*, I almost said. I mean, I don't go around believing in things just to believe in them. I believe in the things that make people free. I believe in the things that bring people to their best lives, that give them the full lives God meant them to have, in good times and bad. Those free lives, those full lives—I've seen them—those are proof of the things I believe. So how could a band of angry, murderous, bitter men like Sherman convince me to believe something else? It was crazy.

I almost said those things out loud, but I didn't. Because I suddenly realized: it was crazy. Everything he was saying was crazy. He seemed to think he had convinced me to become one of the Homelanders. But just as I knew I wouldn't have killed Alex, I knew I never would have become a terrorist. I never would have joined him and his killers, no matter what was happening to me. And yet, they thought I had. Sherman obviously thought I had.

You seemed so committed.

Why? Why did I seem so committed? What had happened to make Sherman think I was one of them?

"You worked on me just like you worked on Alex," I said. "You recruited me to become one of the Homelanders."

"Oh, I told them. I told them," Sherman said. "The situation was just so perfect, it would've been foolish to pass it up." He said this in a kind of whiny, self-defensive voice. It was as if he were arguing with the Homelanders again, trying to convince them to let him recruit me. The argument going on in his mind seemed to make him agitated. He began pacing back and forth in front of me, moving one hand as he talked so that the flashlight beam danced wildly around the room.

I began to shift my legs a little beneath me, began to see if I could maneuver myself into a position to strike.

"I mean, after the police found Alex's blood on your clothing," Sherman went on, excited. "After that, I knew if we just helped them along, if we just . . . supplied the murder weapon with your DNA, we might clinch the deal and get you convicted. It was perfect! A true believer like you! When you saw how unjust everything was—how your precious American system failed you—how God failed you when he didn't send his angels down from heaven to rescue you from being sent to prison—I figured you'd be bitter then, angry, betrayed—the perfect moment for me to get you to see the light. And you did. You did see the light. Better than Alex ever did. You understood everything, just like I thought you would. You were one of us, Charlie. I know you were. You couldn't have been pretending. I told Prince—I told him—but he just wouldn't believe me."

Prince. I knew that name. I'd heard it when the Homelanders captured me. He was their leader. The head of the organization. I was beginning to understand.

"Prince was afraid I was going to betray you like Alex did," I said.

Sherman snorted, getting more agitated, pacing back and forth faster, waving the flashlight around. "Prince!

He was convinced you were working for someone else. He was convinced you were trying to infiltrate us."

The idea sent a thrill of hope through me. Maybe that was the answer. Maybe I was working for someone else, joining the Homelanders only to bring them down. "He thought I was working for the law against you," I said. "He thought I was some kind of spy for the police or something."

I untangled my legs a little more, a little more. Not so much that he would notice, just enough that I'd be able to move quickly.

"I told him that was ridiculous. I told him," Sherman whined.

Of course he had. Because if Sherman had recruited me, and I was some kind of spy, then Sherman was to blame. And I bet when this Prince guy blamed you for something, you didn't survive the experience. So that's why Sherman had come here alone tonight. He was hoping to prove I was innocent, hoping to prove he'd been right to recruit me, right to trust me to become part of his organization. He was hoping to get the information he needed to save himself from Prince's retribution.

Which gave me an idea. Sometimes the simple truth is the best strategy you can come up with.

"I've lost my memory," I told Sherman.

Sherman stopped pacing. He shone the flashlight on me. I saw his eyes gleaming as he stared. "What? What did you say?"

"I never betrayed anybody, Mr. Sherman. I didn't infiltrate anybody. I couldn't get Prince to believe me. I couldn't get anyone to understand. It's not that I'm against you. It's that I just don't remember."

"But how . . . ?"

"I don't know. I don't remember. I don't remember anything. A whole year is gone."

"How can that happen? That doesn't make sense."

"I know . . . but it's true. I didn't betray you, I swear. I just can't remember."

For another moment, Sherman stared, openmouthed. Then I saw his teeth flash in the shadows. He was smiling.

"But that explains it," he said. I could hear the hope in his voice. "That makes sense. You didn't mean to betray us. You just lost your memory—and when you lost your memory, you lost . . ."

"All the work you'd done convincing me."

He gave a little laugh to himself as if in wonder. It was all coming clear to him now. I could practically hear him thinking it through. This explanation might get him off the hook with Prince. If he could convince his leader that I was telling the truth, that I'd lost my memory, then it wouldn't be as if he'd brought a spy into the organization. It wouldn't be his fault.

"They captured me," I said. "They tortured me. But I couldn't tell them anything because I didn't remember. I escaped to stay alive, that's all. If they hadn't tried to kill me, I wouldn't have run."

"Right," said Sherman, still thinking about it. "Right. That makes sense."

"I've just been really confused," I said earnestly—as earnestly as I could. (Beth was right: I could be a pretty decent liar when I put my mind to it.) "Trying to figure out what's right, what's wrong. Trying to figure out who my friends are."

Sherman kind of grunted—that was his only answer. He was still thinking about this, still trying to figure out how he could use it to get himself out of trouble. He was distracted—and that was good. The gun was making him overconfident. But he was standing just a little too far away for me to get to him.

I needed to get him talking again, pacing again if I could.

"In fact, there's something I've really been wondering

about," I said. "Something that doesn't make any sense to me. These Homelander guys—Prince and the rest—they're Islamo-fascists, right? They're trying to make everyone follow their religion. But you don't even believe in God. How come you're working with them?"

He waved this question away with a quick motion of his gun. "I explained this to you a million times, Charlie. A million times."

"I know, but that's what I'm saying. I don't remember."

"We're using them. The Islamos. We're just using them. We have a common goal, so we're working together for the time being." That did it. He got excited again. He started pacing back and forth in front of me again. Waving the flashlight around as he explained. "We both want to bring this country down, drive it into chaos. That's the first step, the all-important step. But once we've achieved that, we'll get rid of them. Because we don't want any more gods. We want a system of fairness, of equality, everyone with the same amount of money, everyone with the same beliefs, no one allowed to say things that offend other people . . ."

He turned and paced back. It brought him closer to me. Almost within reach.

Sherman went on. "Freedom is a mistake, Charlie. Freedom means imperfection. Freedom means inequality and injustice. Freedom means some people getting rich while others don't. When people make their own choices, they make mistakes, they do cruel things. The Islamos want to destroy freedom for their own purposes, for their own way of life. But who cares why they do it as long as they get it done."

He went past me again, a little closer, waving the flashlight, thinking, talking.

"We need them now because they have the commitment and the guns, but as soon as we have this country in flames . . ."

He turned. He paced back. Closer. Close enough.

". . . we'll be able to establish a new . . ."

I tripped him.

It was a dangerous move, but it was the best I could do. With that gun of his waving around, I knew I might catch a bullet, but I also knew he'd kill me eventually anyway.

So I took my chance. I snapped one leg out in front of me. I shot the foot behind his ankle. I brought the other leg back fast and pistoned it out again in a kick to his knee.

The swift pincer move knocked his leg out from under him. The flashlight beam shot into the air as Sherman tumbled over. He went down to the floor. He dropped the light—but not the gun.

I sat forward fast and struck at Sherman's gun hand. At the same moment, he fired.

The blast of the gun was deafening. The flashlight rolled back and forth. The light and shadows expanded and contracted around us, giving the room a bizarre fun-house atmosphere. For a moment, I wasn't sure whether I'd been shot or not.

But no, the bullet had gone wild as the edge of my hand hit Sherman's wrist.

I grabbed his wrist and twisted it. Pressed on his arm, forcing it to the floor, making him cry out in pain.

"Drop it!" I shouted.

He wouldn't. I increased the pressure. His hand finally opened. The gun fell to the floor with a rattling thud.

I shoved Sherman's arm away and snapped up the gun and turned it on him. I scrambled to my feet.

Sherman sat up, rubbing his wrist where I'd twisted it.

The flashlight rolled slowly to a stop, the beam lying across the dusty floor.

Holding the gun on Sherman, I knelt down beside him. I forced my hand into the pocket of his pants and found his car keys. I took them and stood up again out of his reach.

All the while, Sherman stared at me, rubbing his wrist.

"I'm taking you to the police," I said. "You're going to tell them the truth about Alex."

For another second, Sherman stared. Then, slowly, he broke out into a grin. He laughed. The sound sent a chill through me.

"What's so funny?" I said.

"How dumb do you think I am?"

"What do you mean?"

"Did you really think I'd come here alone without some backup, without some insurance?"

I tried to answer his smile with one of my own. "You're alone, all right," I said. But a little sick sensation of doubt rose up in the back of my throat. "There's no one else in this house."

"Oh, you're right about that, Charlie. I couldn't bring anyone with me, because I wasn't sure what you might say. But I know what a dangerous guy you are. I wouldn't just walk in here without a plan B."

He worked his way to his feet.

I gestured at him with the gun. "Take it easy. I'll shoot if I have to."

"You're not gonna shoot, Charlie. In fact, you're going to do exactly what I tell you to do." Smiling, Sherman held his hand out. "And I'm telling you to give me the gun." He saw the doubt in my eyes. His smile got even bigger. And he said, "Give me the gun, Charlie—or Beth dies."

Rage flashed through me like a flame. Before I even knew what I was doing, I grabbed Sherman by the front of his shirt and slammed him back against the wall. I stuck the gun into his face.

"What are you talking about? Where is she?" I pressed the gun hard into his cheek, my finger tightening on the trigger. My voice came out hoarse and ferocious through my gritted teeth. "Is Beth in danger? Tell me! Tell me! You think I won't kill you? Don't be stupid. I'll kill you, all right. Where is she?"

He still managed to smile, even with the gun barrel digging into him. "Oh, she's fine, Charlie. She's sitting at home. She's doing her homework. Her parents are out for the evening. She's all by herself, working at the computer in her bedroom upstairs. And in approximately five minutes, if my people don't hear from me, they're going to pay her a little visit. They'll come in oh-so-quietly, Charlie. She won't even know they're there. And they'll kill her quietly, too, a knife to the throat. Cutting deep so she can't cry out. She'll bleed to death on the floor without a sound. No one'll even know it happened until her parents get home and find her."

I was so angry I wanted to kill him then and there. So angry I could barely speak, but I managed it. "You're going to call them. Your people. You're going to phone them now and call them off."

Sherman laughed. "Am I? Or am I going to call them and say a code word that starts them going. How will you know, Charlie? How will you know?"

When he saw that I had no answer, he gave another hard chuckle.

"Face it, Charlie. You're tougher than I am, but I'm a lot smarter than you. You have no choice. It's you or Beth. Give me back the gun."

To be honest, I don't know what I would've done if I'd been thinking clearly. Maybe I just would've surrendered to save Beth. Maybe that's what I should've done. But my fury against this man—this man who had murdered my friend—this man who had stolen my life from me—who was threatening to kill Beth—that fury roared through me hotter than ever, and I hit him. Without even thinking, I drew back the gun and smashed the butt of it into the side of his head.

I was still gripping his shirtfront in my other hand and I felt him become a dead weight as he lost consciousness. I let him go. He dropped to the floor.

For a moment, I stared at him where he lay. As my mind cleared, I realized what I'd done. Now he couldn't make the call, couldn't pull off his goons. They would break into Beth's house in five minutes and kill her.

Frantically, I looked around the room. I had to think, I had to think. In the outglow of the flashlight, I saw the laptop on the floor. I saw the cell phone. I grabbed them.

I would need them if I was going to save Beth's life.

CHAPTER TWENTY-NINE

Five Minutes

Sherman's car was parked just down the path from the house. I saw it in the early moonlight: a sleek, silver BMW.

I rushed to it, stumbling sloppily over the pebbles and loose dirt under my shoes. I jumped behind the wheel, tossing the laptop onto the passenger seat beside me. I flipped the laptop open and brought it out of sleep mode. While it woke up, I jammed the car key into the ignition and started the engine.

There was so much I needed to do, and it all had to be

done at once. I needed to get to Beth's house to protect her. That was the first thing because I wasn't far and I could probably get to her before the police. But I needed to call the police too. And even before that, I needed to warn Beth, to tell her to get out of the house before Sherman's killers came for her.

I tapped the webcam icon on the laptop and brought Beth's computer up onto the screen.

I flipped the car into gear and stepped down on the gas.

I felt the tires spit pebbles out behind me. Then the rubber gripped the dirt and the Beamer shot forward. The car bounced and bounded toward the mansion's gate.

I glanced over at the laptop. She had her camera on. I saw the webcam image of Beth's room on the monitor. I could see her bed against one wall with big pillows and a stuffed alligator on it. I could see her closet at the head of the bed, the door open, clothes hanging inside. I could see her dresser against the other wall under a bulletin board crowded over every inch with snapshots. I could see the door with a cross to one side of it and a poster of a window with a green field outside on the other.

But Beth herself was not in sight.

The BMW sped through the dark along the dirt path,

shuddering and skidding. The headlights speared the deep shadows under the trees. I went for the cell phone in my fleece pocket. Held it to me, snapped it open with my thumb. Driving clumsily with one hand, I had to struggle to keep the car from veering to the left or right, from smashing into the trunk of one of the trees along the path.

Josh had programmed all my friends' numbers into the phone. I pressed 1 with my thumb. I dialed Beth.

As I waited for the phone to ring, I saw the iron gate up ahead that led out to the public road. Luckily, Sherman had left the gate open. I held the wheel firmly with one hand, guiding the car over the rough path, aiming it for the open gate.

The phone rang in my ear—and at the same time, the car went through the gate, bouncing out onto the bad road beyond. The car wiggled under me, trying to skid on the broken macadam. I wrestled it straight with my one hand, holding the phone to my ear with the other.

The phone rang again—and then I heard Beth's singing ring tone come echoing back to me over the laptop's speaker. I glanced at the monitor. I couldn't see it, but her phone was in her room somewhere, the sound of it coming over the microphone in her computer as it rang.

But where was Beth?

The phone rang again. There was no sign of her. I remembered Sherman's sneering threat.

They'll kill her quietly, too, a knife to the throat. Cutting deep so she can't cry out. She'll bleed to death on the floor without a sound.

Horrible images came into my mind. Maybe I was too late. Maybe Sherman's thugs had already come into the house and . . .

I took my eyes off the road, glanced at the computer again—and now I saw Beth's door start to open. I glanced from the monitor to the windshield and back again. And then I saw Beth herself step into the room.

I breathed a deep sigh of relief. She looked all right, perfectly fine, good, wearing jeans and a sweater, calm, relaxed. They hadn't gotten to her.

As I glanced over again, I saw her find her ringing cell phone lying on the bed. She looked at the number on the readout and picked it up.

"Charlie?"

"Come to the computer, Beth. Talk to me through there."

"What's wrong?"

"Do it."

I snapped the phone shut and slipped it back into my pocket. Now I could drive with both hands and talk to her through the computer.

I felt the road grow more solid under me as I drove quickly through a run-down neighborhood on the outskirts of town.

"Charlie?"

Beth's voice sounded small and tinny now as she spoke to me through the computer.

I glanced over at her. Her face loomed large as she stared through the monitor at me.

"Beth, listen to me. It was Sherman. Sherman killed Alex."

"Mr. Sherman?"

"He's sent people to your house."

"What? I don't understand. Why . . . ?"

"To hurt you. To kill you, Beth. You need to get out— and then you need to call the police. But get out first —now—carefully—make sure no one's waiting for you. Get out and call the police. Don't ask questions. Just do it."

"All right, all right."

I came to a stop sign. I wanted to rush through it, but I was afraid of the police. If they pulled me over, I would never get to her. By the time I convinced them Beth was in danger, it might be too late.

I slowed the car just enough, then stepped on the gas again, coming around the corner onto Morgan Drive, a large boulevard with four lanes of two-way traffic. There weren't many cars out tonight, but there was a steady flow in both directions. I had to keep a careful eye on the road.

I kept stealing glances over at the laptop. There was Beth. She was moving toward the door. I urged her on in my mind: *Get out of there. Get out.*

But then she stopped. I saw her freeze, tense, one hand uplifted. She had left the bedroom door open when she came in. Now she was staring through it, out into the hall, out to the top of the stairs just visible on the computer monitor.

"Beth . . ." I said.

At the sound of my voice, she glanced back at the computer, back at me. She put her finger to her lips. Her voice came softly through the computer.

"Ssh. I think someone's in the house."

"Are you sure?" I said, trying to keep my voice down. I hated to think that her time had run out, that she couldn't get away.

She shook her head quickly. She wasn't sure. Putting her finger to her lips again, she moved to the door to listen better.

I drove quickly down the boulevard, weaving through the traffic, glancing over at the scene on the computer. It was like watching a horror movie, like watching the suspenseful scene where the heroine is caught in the house with the killer. I felt that afraid, that helpless to do anything about what was happening onscreen.

Only this wasn't a movie. It was real. It was Beth. And I needed to get to her.

Beth stood listening. Finally, I couldn't take the tension anymore.

"Beth!" I said in a hoarse whisper. "Shut the door. Lock the door. Call the police. Dial 911."

A horn blared loudly. I looked to the windshield just in time to see I had let the BMW drift across the center line. A pair of headlights was lancing toward me. I wrestled the wheel to the right, wrestled the car to the right, back into my lane, out of the headlights' path. The oncoming car raced by me.

Now there was a traffic light up ahead. It turned from green to yellow as I approached. I jammed my foot down on the gas and sped through it.

Finally I had a chance to glance over at the laptop again. There was Beth. She hadn't heard me. She had crept out through the doorway into the upstairs hall, walking softly. I could tell by her posture she was listening, listening to see if anyone had come into the house.

"Beth!" I said. "Get back in your room. Lock the door."

But even as I spoke, I heard it. Even there, in the car, the sound reached me through the computer's speakers.

A floorboard creaked in Beth's house. Someone was coming up the stairs.

Watching the busy road ahead, grabbing looks at the monitor, I saw Beth freeze in her tracks in the upstairs hallway. I saw her turn back to look at her bedroom door, to look at her computer, to look at me. Her mouth was open. Her eyes were wide with fear.

"Beth!" I whispered harshly. "Get back!"

I gestured to her—to the computer. I waved frantically to get her to come back into the room.

Finally, she moved. Hurrying on tiptoe, she dashed back down the hall, back into her bedroom. She closed the door quietly. There was a little twist knob, a bolt lock. She turned it. It wouldn't keep anyone out for long, but it might slow them down. Sherman had told me they didn't want to make any noise. They wanted to come and go quietly—come and kill her quietly and go. I didn't think they would just blast through the lock with a gunshot.

At least, I hoped they wouldn't.

I saw Beth standing in the center of the room. I started to speak, to tell her again to dial the police. But before I could, she flipped open the phone. Dialed 911.

She called for help. So did I: I prayed desperately as I peered through the windshield, working the steering wheel, forcing the car to weave left around a slow-moving van, then back quickly into the right lane to avoid a car that had paused for a left turn at an intersection. I prayed: *Not her, Lord. Me. Not her.*

"Police?" I could hear over the laptop speaker how shaky Beth's voice was, how scared she was. Well, I was scared too. I was only a couple of minutes away, but it felt like a million miles. I felt completely helpless to reach her. I heard her say, "My name is Beth Summers. I live at 45 Madison. There's someone in my house. Please send help. What? No. Someone in my house. Please, please . . ." She was close to tears.

And then she cried out.

I looked over at the laptop and saw the phone fall from

her hand. Now I heard what she heard: a sound at the door. Trembling, Beth turned slowly to face it. The sound came again. A soft rattle. Glancing from the road in front of me to the laptop on the seat beside me, I saw the doorknob start to turn slowly, this way and that. Staring, terrified, Beth stumbled back a step.

It was hard to tear my eyes away, but I had to. I had to face front again. There was my next turn up ahead. I was almost there. It was a left turn and I was in the right lane. There was traffic to the side of me and traffic coming toward me. Somehow I had to get around all of it.

I twisted the steering wheel hard. The BMW squealed. The Volkswagen beside me screeched and skidded. An oncoming Cadillac sent up a blast of its horn. I cut recklessly across the lanes and shot off Morgan onto Belmont, a smaller, darker side street.

I stepped on the gas and raced into shadows. Madison—Beth's street—was only four blocks ahead.

Now I could spare a glance back at the laptop. Beth still stood frozen where she was, still staring at the door.

The knob was turning faster now, harder. The door started to rattle.

"Beth," I said.

My voice startled her. She spun toward me in terror.

"The window!" I said. "Can you get out the window?"

She shook her head frantically. "Too high. I'll break my leg. They'll catch me."

She jumped as a loud bang came through the door. They were going to kick it in.

"A weapon, Beth. Find a weapon. A baseball bat. A hockey stick."

"I don't have any . . ."

"A shoe. A high-heeled shoe. Anything. Hold them off. I'm almost there."

Beth cried out in fear again as, again, the killers kicked the door.

"A weapon!" I said.

But I had to face forward, had to steer the car as it raced through the darkness under a canopy of trees.

There was Washington Street up ahead. Madison Street was next.

"Oh please!" I whispered—and pressed down on the gas, pushing the car at speed through the empty intersection.

There was another bang against Beth's door just as I glanced back at the monitor. I saw the door jolt in its frame. It was breaking. They were getting through.

But now, Beth forced herself out of her frozen terror.

She rushed to the closet. She shoved aside some clothes. She reached in deeper and when she came out, I saw she had an iron in her hand—a regular old iron for pressing clothes.

"Oh yes!" I said.

Beth was slender. She wasn't athletic. She wasn't strong. But an iron—that'll stop a man. And I was almost there.

"Get to where the door opens," I said. "Get to where they'll come through. Swing for the head the second you see them. Don't hesitate."

Beth was so scared now she was crying, trembling, sobbing. But she found the courage to do what I said. She moved to the door just as the killers kicked it again. She flinched at the sound, but all the same, she positioned herself at the place where the door would open. She gripped the handle of the iron with one hand and gripped her wrist with the other, holding the iron down low at her side, ready to swing.

And just then, before I could see what happened next, I reached the house.

I hit the Beamer's brakes hard, turned the wheel hard, and the car swerved to the curb and screeched to a halt.

The next second, I was out the door, running like a madman up the path to Beth's front door.

The killers had left the door unlatched, but it wouldn't have mattered. If it had been locked, I'd've smashed right through.

Now I was in the house. I was bounding up the stairs, two at a time. I was in the upstairs hallway . . .

And there was another loud bang, a rending crash. I crested the stairs just in time to see the killers break through Beth's door.

There were two of them. Big men dressed in black. The one who'd kicked the door in rushed through before I could get there. The other was already crowding in behind him.

I heard Beth scream—and I saw her as she stepped into the doorway, as she swung the iron at the lead man with all the strength she had.

The blow hit the killer smack in the side of the head. His mouth flew open. He toppled to the floor, falling forward with his own onrushing force.

But the second killer didn't hesitate. He had Beth in an instant. He grabbed her arm, twisted it, forcing her to drop the iron. With the other hand he slapped her hard across the face, once and then again.

I was running toward him down the hall. I saw him shift his grip to grab Beth by the front of her sweater. I saw his other hand go to his waist. It all happened so fast, while Beth was still dazed by his blows.

The killer's hand came up in the air. I saw the knife raised above Beth's face.

A sound came out of me then—a sound I'd never heard myself make before. It wasn't a karate kee-yai or a shout or a scream or anything like that. It was a wild, enormous, guttural roar of pure animal fury.

Before the killer struck, I had him. I grabbed him by the belt and by the collar. I'd heard stories like this—stories about someone who became so desperate or so angry or so afraid, they did something superhuman: lifted a bus to save a child or outraced an avalanche or something amazing like that.

I tore the killer off Beth by main strength and hoisted him in the air—hoisted him clear above my head as if he were nothing more than a stuffed dummy.

Roaring, I threw him, just that easily. I hurled him headlong down the hall.

The killer's body went spinning through the air. He landed with a thud that shook the floor, just a few yards away from me. The jar of the fall made him lose his hold on the knife, but he quickly grabbed it again. He scrambled to his feet right away.

But not fast enough. Not fast enough by a long shot.

I was already there. I don't even remember moving. It was that quick. I was there in front of him.

He slashed at me with the knife, backhand. I dodged away. The blade went past. I stepped in quickly and blocked his arm as it came swinging back toward me. At the same time, I punched him in the throat. His eyes bulged. His tongue came out. He gagged. I grabbed his wrist—the hand holding the knife. I twisted it around and brought my arm down on his elbow as hard as I could. The killer's arm broke with a loud, sickening snap. He let out a single strangled scream and dropped to the floor, unconscious.

His knife lay beside him, just beyond his fingertips. I swept it up. I dropped to one knee. I grabbed the unconscious man by the shirtfront, hauled him up off the floor. I raised the knife over my head, ready to plunge it into his body as he lay there helpless.

Oh, and I wanted to do it too. I have to be honest. I really did want to. I was thinking about the way he'd slapped Beth, the way he'd grabbed her and was going to kill her. The rage was inside me, filling me, pushing me, as if I were a puppet being worked by a giant hand.

But I wasn't a puppet. I had a choice. Sensei Mike

wasn't there to stop me anymore, but he was there, and God was there, and I had a choice.

My hand, holding the knife, trembled in the air, but I didn't bring it down. I wouldn't bring it down.

I let out a noise of frustration and threw the knife down the hall. I released my hold on the unconscious killer and let him fall with a thud to the floor.

The whole thing took a second, maybe two. Then I was on my feet, rushing back to Beth where she slumped against the doorframe. She was holding her jaw where the killer had slapped her, blinking hard, trying to fight her way out of her daze.

I glanced down at the floor, at the first killer, the one she'd hit with the iron. He was out cold. I smiled. Nice one, Beth.

I took her gently by the shoulders, lifted her away from the doorframe.

"Come on," I said. "Let's get out of here."

And now—again—I heard the sirens.

CHAPTER THIRTY

Into the Night

I took Beth by the hand and led her around the fallen body of the killer, led her to the stairs and down to the front door.

"You're hurt," I heard her say softly behind me.

I glanced at my arm. She was right. The killer had cut me when he slashed with the knife. There was blood soaking through the sleeve of my fleece.

"It'll be okay," I told her.

We pushed out into the fresh air of the autumn night.

The sirens sounded louder outside. They were close, though I still couldn't see the lights.

I turned to face Beth, holding her hand. She lifted her face to me. Her eyes were clear now, clear and soft and kind. She was the Beth I knew.

"I have to go," I told her.

"Don't," she said. "You can't. You're hurt. You need a doctor."

She gripped my hand tighter and took my other hand too. I raised her hands to my lips and kissed them.

"I have to. The police. You hear them?" The sirens grew louder in the night. I looked into her eyes. "Tell them, Beth. Tell them it was Sherman. Tell them he's the one who killed Alex, who sent these men. Tell them to go to the Ghost Mansion. I left him there. Tell them what happened tonight."

"Stay, Charlie. You can tell them yourself. They'll believe you now. They have to."

"I can't. It'll be his word against mine—and I'm a convicted killer. I can't take the chance they'll arrest me again. There's something I have to do. Someone I have to find."

"No. No. You're hurt . . ."

"Beth . . ."

"Please," she said. Her eyes filled with tears. "I'm so scared for you. Every day. I'm so scared. Don't go."

I wrapped my arms around her. I held her close to me. I pressed the side of my face against hers and felt her tears on my cheek. I heard the sirens grow louder and louder. Would they ever stop? Would they ever stop chasing me?

I whispered quickly into Beth's ear, "I'm sorry. I'm so sorry. But I have to do this. I have to go. I think I know who I am now. I think I was sent to do something, something important. I have to find the man who sent me. I have to do what he sent me to do."

"Why?" she burst out angrily. She was crying hard now. "Why does it have to be you, Charlie? Why do you have to leave me again? Why do you have to fight? Why do you have to be hunted and hated and shot at and hurt? Why can't it be someone else?"

For another moment, I held her as close as I could. I tried to keep the feel of her in my mind and the smell of her and the sound of her voice so I could remember it all in the days to come when I was alone.

"Why does it have to be you?" she said again.

"Because," I told her, "I'm the good guys."

But now, the red glow of the police cars' lights shone

on the canopy of trees down the street. The headlights of the cruisers appeared, racing toward us.

Using all my willpower, I pushed Beth away, letting only my hands linger on her shoulders. I looked down into her eyes.

"Thank you," I said. "Tell Josh and Rick and Miler—tell them I said thank you."

She nodded. I could see it was hard for her, but she did. "I will," she whispered. And then she forced herself to say, "You'd better hurry."

"I don't want to let you go."

"I know. I don't want you to. But they're coming. You have to leave."

I took my hands off her. I never wanted to do it, never. It broke my heart.

We looked at each other as the red lights of the cruisers played over us.

"I will come back, Beth," I said. "God is my witness."

She tried her best to smile. She whispered, "Run, Charlie. Run."

And I did.

CPSIA information can be obtained at www.ICGtesting.com
Printed in the USA
LVOW051110270911

248043LV00024B/2/P